ANNA WITH TRISTRAM

Anna With Tristram

a novel by
Gwendolen Freeman

BREWIN BOOKS

First published by
Brewin Books, Studley, Warwickshire, B80 7LG
in August 1996

© Copyright Gwendolen Freeman 1996

All rights reserved

ISBN 1 85858 028 5

British Library Cataloguing in Publication Data
A Catalogue record for this book is available from the British Library

All rights reserved. No part of this book may be reproduced, stored on a retrieval system, or transmitted in any form or by any means, electronic, electrostatic, magnetic tape, mechanical, photocopying, recording or otherwise without prior permission in writing from Gwendolen Freeman, the copyright owner.

Typeset in Plantin by
Avon Dataset Ltd, Bidford on Avon, Warks, B50 4JH
Printed by Supaprint (Redditch) Limited, Redditch.

BY THE SAME AUTHOR

The Houses Behind (Allen & Unwin 1947)
Children Never Tell (Allen & Unwin 1949)
When You Are Old (Allen & Unwin 1951)
The Last Kings of Thule – a translation of the French book by Jean Malaurie (Allen & Unwin 1956)
Between Two Worlds – a book of verse (Outposts 1978)
The Leavises – The first essay (Cambridge University Press 1984)
A Zeppelin in My Childhood (Charles Skilton 1989)
United Family Record (Brewin 1989)
Alma Mater (Girton College 1990)
Scriptural Beasts (Charles Skilton 1991)
World of an Artist (Brewin 1991)
Ways of Loving (Brewin 1993)
The Dodona Oak (Brewin 1995)

ANNA WITH TRISTRAM

It was a warm late afternoon in October, a day when winter seemed far away. Anna, sitting at her high Fleet Street window, thought it might offer something not yet known but delightful. She had asked Tristram Forrest to come and discuss his work, and now she looked down at the thronged street with its line of traffic and people congregating at bus-stops, and her heart fluttered. He, the unknown, was somewhere down there.

Sometimes she could hardly believe that she belonged to this rushing London. She had been in it less than three months, and before that had been only on brief visits. But Dad, who ran the small family works in Birmingham, had happened to know the accountant of the *Staffordshire Echo*, and had heard that the paper was launching a London Letter for Women. Anna was small with fair hair, and at twenty-two looked, people said, like a sixteen-year-old. She also had no experience of commercial journalism. On the other hand she came from a local family, had been head girl at her school and had just obtained a good English degree. She had, as well, helped to edit an undergraduate magazine.

She went for an interview with hazy ideas of what she wanted to do in life; was told that she was too young, but had then been offered the post. Dad had said that she was not old enough to set up in a flat on her own in London, but her mother, who had been a campaigner for women's rights, thought she should try if she wanted to. The London editor's wife found her a flat above a stationer's shop near Waterloo Station, and now she was 'little Miss Dean' at the Fleet Street office.

She had to provide five paragraphs a day on subjects supposed to interest women. Most of them she wrote herself, reporting on meetings and exhibitions, but she was allowed to use some outside material. The friendly men at the office sent up pieces that they thought possible, and now the London editor had found this short rhapsody, 'Girl in a Rose Garden' by Tristram Forrest. But the editor could not have read it, for it had nothing to do with the London world and no information.

It was the description of a young girl standing on a terrace above a rose garden at night. She had no name nor personality. She was a symbol. She was looking at the dark summer garden with its trees against the sky and breathing the scent and wondering about the world with its battles and cruelties, and she was afraid. As she stood on the terrace she said goodbye to childhood and looked with dread on the future. But then the scent of the roses, the stars and the trees reassured her that there must be some ultimate goodness in creation. She turned and went through the dark door behind her.

The girl was not, Anna thought, a typical figure. Most adolescents did not dread the future but wanted to grow up. But the piece was like a prose poem with sentences like music. She was moved, dazzled. She must see the writer.

Anna's mother called her the 'lieutenant colonel'. She was known for her energy. She made resolutions and kept them. She sent the piece back with a note to this Tristram Forrest asking if he would like to come and discuss his work. She had no idea what she would say to him, but already she had a faint feeling that he would be part of her life.

A note written in a fine italic hand was left at the office. Addressing her as 'Dear Madam', Tristram Forrest thanked her for her invitation. He would call at five on Friday, hoping that her work would be finished for the day.

The formality oppressed her a little. He might be a greybeard or a stout family father. But all that Friday she was vaguely excited, and she took her paragraphs early to the wire room that communicated with the Staffordshire headquarters.

He was punctual. She heard the voice of Kathleen, the friendly girl behind the office counter downstairs, and a man's voice sounding light and cultured thanking her. A tap came at the door, and Anna got up and turned.

There is generally disappointment in meeting an author. He is human with human peculiarities, not a voice. But this Tristram Forrest was, Anna thought, a poetic-looking figure – young, slight and dark-haired with fine features and soft brown eyes. And, seeing him, she had the absolute certainty that in some way they would be linked.

He came forward hesitantly. It seemed to Anna that they were playing some game, pretending that they did not know one another. But she had to play the editor. She said formally, 'I enjoyed your writing, but I'm afraid it's unsuitable for a provincial daily.'

He said politely that he would be grateful for criticism. It was the first time that he had tried anything for newspapers.

She wanted to know more about him. 'You're a teacher?'

'I've recently returned from Paris.'

'France!' she said delighted. 'You should have lots of interesting things to write about.'

'I don't really know anything about politics or trade figures,' he said. She was to find that it was his habit to depreciate himself.

'No, but you could write on life in France. Only you would want some peg to make it topical.'

She who had been a journalist for fewer than three months was giving advice as if she had had years of experience. But in Tristram, she was also to find later, there was something – a modesty, a gentle attention that drew people out. Unlike other people, he had not appeared surprised at her youthfulness.

She asked, 'Why did you send us your piece?'

'I was going up to St Paul's, and I saw your gold letters. They shine out on a wet day.'

That too was to prove typical – his impractical reason for an action. His unworldliness seemed to Anna charming. She would have liked to ask more, but he had turned to the door. She said hastily, 'If you would like to bring something else in I could try it on the Staffordshire office. They have a column article on the leader page.'

'Staffordshire office', 'leader page' – they had nothing to do with Tristram. But he said politely, 'Thank you very much. I'll try.'

'There's a file of the paper in the downstairs office. You could have a look at it.' Then she thought of the spiked pile of greyish close-printed paper with its columns of local crime, property markets, road accidents, council meetings, and it seemed ludicrous to introduce Tristram to it. She said, 'Journalism is very cheap, of course. You ought to write a book.'

But he did not respond to this invitation to more talk. His hand was on the door, and for the first time she experienced the pain of parting which was to darken her life later. She saw that she could not keep him and asked, 'Shall I show you out?'

'No, thankyou. I can find my way.'

She said, 'Good luck' and the door closed. She lay back fatigued, half-happy, half-disturbed with feelings that she could not control. She did not want to control them. She wanted to remember his face.

Rose, sitting in the lecture hall with its group of middle-aged serious people – social workers, businessmen, clergy – only half listened to the speakers. The meeting was to discuss the immigrants that, twenty years after the war, were still streaming into Britain, particularly into the Midland towns. The meeting agreed that the problem was urgent, but Rose had her own problem.

'Shall I go? Shan't I go?' The question raged on as one speaker after another mounted the platform. She had to think not only of herself but of Edward to whom she had grown devoted. There was no secret in her devotion to him and the family. She was always thanking them, but she did not know how much they depended on her.

She had never been sure. It had been just kindness at first when she had come to see them after the death of her mother. She would have liked to stay on in Ladyhill, the Worcestershire village, permanently, but Edward had urged her to train for a career, and she had not known even then if it had been thought for her welfare or the desire to get rid of her. She had not a very high opinion of herself though she seemed to make friends easily.

She had been lucky in a way. She had taken the social-work course in Birmingham and then got a job locally so that she could visit Ladyhill regularly at week-ends. She felt now that Edward depended on her. Things had changed at The Hollies, and Helena, the sister whom he had guarded for years, had married and had a child, so Edward no longer had the responsibility. He had reacted rather oddly, saying that he was leading too easy and narrow a life, though he still had his gardens to run, still gave a few piano lessons and took part in village affairs. He was in his sixties and had a rheumatic knee, but he still seemed to feel that he was over-privileged.

Each week-end Rose had been reporting on her work, which brought her into contact with the poor and deprived. Edward listened carefully and even sometimes sent small gifts of money to people for whom he was sorry. But now a choice had come. Rose had been offered a more responsible job in Yorkshire. She was a Londoner. She did not know the North. And she did not want to leave Edward. Yet he urged her to go.

She thought that he was being unselfish and did not really wish to lose her. If she went there would be nobody to give him news of the world of poverty outside Ladyhill, nobody to discuss social problems. Helena was busy with her books on Midland history and her child. Jos, her husband, was busy with his pottery and the gardens in which he helped Edward. Benedict, the boy, was away at Cambridge and taking a classics degree which hardly touched social problems of the 1960s. 'If I go,' Rose thought, 'he'll sit by himself after Saturday supper and feel cut off from the world.' She had been considering her friends. Was there anybody whom she could ask to call? But they were all busy and not known in Ladyhill.

A Pakistani on the platform was talking of the insults that he had endured from the public, and Rose gave him her attention for a moment, thinking that her own problems were small compared with his. He told a story of a woman accusing him of keeping a harem, and the woman beside Rose caught her eye and smiled. She was amused at something – the man's clipped speech, the solemn faces of his listeners or just the ridiculous incident.

Rose had come in a little late and sat at the end of a row of chairs. The woman beside her was elderly, with short white hair, a wide generous mouth and a thin figure. Once or twice she looked at her watch. She was married, probably with household duties.

The meeting was going on for too long. Some cleric was now on the platform, repeating that he would arrange a meeting at his parish hall. A door opened at the back of the room, and girls appeared with trays of cups, but still he went on talking.

The woman beside Rose whispered 'May I?' and stood up. Rose moved to let her pass and then on an impulse decided to follow her. They went through a side door into a corridor, and the woman said grimacing, 'The voice of the turtle is heard in our land.'

She had a sharp tongue then. Rose asked, 'Are you in a hurry to get anywhere?'

'Only home. Edgbaston. I have a husband and son to see to.'

'I've got a car.'

'Oh no thanks. I can catch a bus.'

But when they looked out the rush-hour had begun and traffic was streaming by. Rose said, 'Come on. I've finished for the day,' and they went together to the car park and exchanged names. The woman was Agnes Dean, who did part-time welfare work among employees of her small family factory. 'I began before I was twenty. I've seen a lot of changes.'

The traffic was very thick. It took them nearly half an hour to reach the Dean home in a side road of red Edwardian houses. It was a modest semi-detached building with some neat bushes in the small front garden. 'Dad,' Mrs Dean said, 'unwinds over the garden.'

'Dad' came to the door – a small man with a moustache and a Birmingham accent, hardly Rose would have thought a match for Mrs Dean. But they seemed fond of one another as he said, 'The kettle's on' and she apologised for being late.

After this Rose could not refuse a cup of tea. They sat in a family room with a well-worn carpet and mixed chairs but with books in a corner. It was Dad who brought in the tea while Mrs Dean took off her coat and talked. It was mainly about the problems she had known before the war. She had lost her parents in childhood and had been brought up by her grandparents who owned the factory. They were Unitarians and 'serious and progressive', she said.

Now and then Dad added a remark. He had come from a poor home and worked up to be a manager in the factory. 'Aggie,' he said, 'had a lot of young men after her. I never knew why she took me.'

In the middle a round-faced boy with golden-brown hair came in and was introduced as 'Hughie who loves cars'. He ate a large tea but said nothing and vanished, and Dad took out the tray and left the two women together. Rose said several times that she must go, but the talk continued. Mrs Dean asked after Rose's work, and Rose said, 'I don't know.'

The problem came out in the end, and it included the story of Rose's relations with Ladyhill. Mrs Dean asked, 'That's not the Helena Carey who writes books on Midland history, is it?'

'Yes. She's Edward's sister but she's married now. She was with me at Cambridge.'

'You're lucky to know them.' But Rose shook her head. 'I'm worried about Edward.'

Mrs Dean commented, 'Partings are inevitable you know. I've just lost a daughter who's become a journalist in Fleet Street.'

They talked on. It was after seven when Rose at last got up. In the last few minutes an idea had come to her, and she said, 'Would you like to meet the Careys?'

That evening she telephoned to Edward. He asked, 'What about Yorkshire?'

'I haven't decided, but Edward I've met a charming woman and I thought you might like to see her.'

'Haven't I got enough charming women already?' he said joking.

But Rose persisted. 'She could come out on Saturday afternoon while her husband is watching TV sport.'

Since Helena's marriage The Hollies had grown used to visitors. People came to see the gardens. Others interested in Jos's pottery looked in. Jenny Owen from the stores walked up to play with the child Irene. Village people came on local affairs. But no visitor except Rose herself knew much about the back streets of cities.

6

Anna With Tristram

When Rose said, 'She does part-time work at some small family factory' Edward sounded pleased. 'Splendid. We can discuss suicide and abortion and lung cancer.' He was still making jokes.

Actually that Saturday afternoon when Mrs Dean came out there was a flood of conversation. She was an amusing talker and she knew a great deal about social problems, but her chief quality, Rose thought, was an entire lack of façade. If she said something it was the truth as she knew it. She had no romantic illusions except possibly about her children, and she hardly mentioned them except to say that she had a clever daughter in London and a boy of seventeen at home who was slow in growing up. She talked about Birmingham history and its changing problems – unemployment in the early thirties, the struggle to have family planning accepted and then the war. 'Anna was a baby but I couldn't leave Dad on his own. We only had some windows broken.'

Rose and Helena left the two talking while they got the tea. As she went to and fro Rose heard earnest argument.

'But the very effort of coping with hardship . . .'

'It doesn't automatically make you a better person, you know, Mr Carey . . .'

Talk continued at tea, and then Mrs Dean suddenly got up and said, 'Heavens. I didn't know it was so late.' As she left Edward said, 'Come again when you can,' and to Rose, 'She's fiercer than you, my dear, but she's good.'

Before Rose left on the Sunday Edward asked, 'Still thinking about Yorkshire?'

'Oh, I suppose I'll go,' Rose said.

It was Anna's last address. For three Saturdays she had tramped round Southwark looking for women who had disappeared. The task had been given her by the local settlement, and now she had to find only Miss Louise Sparrow.

The flat area south of Waterloo Station had changed since the war. The noisy street markets had gone and bombs had made open spaces. But the local settlement remained in a terrace lining a quiet square. It had always been supported by women, and Anna had heard of it in her student days. During her romantic adolescence she had decided to do good in the world, and in her early months in

London, when she knew few people and had abundant spare time, she had gone to the settlement to offer her services.

The brisk woman at the settlement seemed pleased to see her. Anna could have helped with a club, but she had one disadvantage. Attending meetings and exhibitions at any time of the day, she never knew quite when she would be free. However there was a small job that she could do, the woman said. The settlement ran a club for women, but through the years some of the members had disappeared. Would Anna trace them and persuade them to come back?

With a list of names and addresses Anna had wandered during September in that characterless area with its dirty brick blocks. In Birmingham the poor lived in courts, but in London they lived on top of one another. She went up bare wooden stairs smelling of cats and stale food and came on dishevelled women speaking a Cockney language that she did not always understand. She had not been very lucky in her search. Some of the women on her list had gone away. Some could not be traced at all. Only two had said that they would return to the club. Now she was at her last address.

It was a low brick building beside a railway arch. Old and dirty with cracked slates, it yet had a door half open. Inside were the usual bare dusty stairs, and an old woman emerged from a side room and said, in answer to Anna's question, "Er's upstairs.'

Above was a bare landing with a stained sink and dripping tap. A dusty clogged window revealed two doors facing one another. Both doors were open, but on the right a high armchair with a pile of garments on the back almost blocked the entrance. Protruding from the side was a claw hand.

A small woman with glasses, trailing grey hair and a soiled apron came out from behind the chair. 'What you want?'

Anna said that the settlement had sent her to look for Miss Louise Sparrow.

'That's 'er,' the woman said nodding at the chair. Anna edged round and saw a long emaciated figure with a white face and drooping head. It was dressed in a ragged dark shawl and a blanket, and from the bent head a thread of saliva descended. Anna said, 'You used to belong to the settlement, didn't you?' and the figure made a harsh sound but Anna could not tell what it said.

The room had an old gas-stove, a rusty grate without a fire, a tattered mat and a ragged curtain presumably hiding a bed. There was little else but an old table, a wooden chair and some boxes.

The woman attendant said, 'Parkinson's disease. Looks as though she could get to a club, don't she?'

The figure in the chair made another confused sound, and the old woman said, 'She wants to do a wee.' Anna hauled up the gaunt figure that seemed to weigh a ton, and the old woman brought a chamber-pot. It was a difficult exercise and needed strong arms. When the figure was dropped back into her chair, the old woman seemed to have decided that Anna was a friend. She said, 'Used to be a smart woman. Now she can't even get to bed. It's hard to manage.'

'But somebody helps you?'

'The woman below comes up, but she don't like it.'

'And food?'

'We pay a kid across the road to do some shopping. But she don't like it neither. I gets out when I can, but my eyes ain't what they was.'

The figure in the chair again said something, and the old woman translated. She says ask the settlement to get her an oil stove. Her chimney smokes.'

Cold seemed the last misery. Anna asked, 'What does the doctor say?'

The old woman led her into her own room opposite. It was dirty but not quite as dirty, and there was a small fire. She began to pour out a flood of confidences now that the figure in the chair could not hear. 'I'm Mrs Dot Noakes, and I've been 'ere almost since the war. Things was terrible then, but people was more friendly. Now it's darn hard to get help from anybody.'

'But your doctor?'

'She ain't got no doctor.'

'But you must have.'

'No dear. She didn't bother.'

Anna asked, 'Can I do anything?'

'Well dear, if you could get us a few fags . . .'

Anna went down the stairs and out to the street. It was like returning to the normal world from a hidden horror. She meditated on Miss Sparrow as she went round the small shops. She, Anna, was the 'lieutenant colonel' who got things done. It was no good going to the settlement. It knew nothing of Miss Sparrow. The best thing would be to contact a hospital.

She bought cigarettes and a pile of tinned foods. The stairs were dark, but a light with an unshaded bulb had been switched on above and glared on the bare wooden floor of the landing. The figure was quiet in its chair, but Mrs Noakes was warming her hands over her small smoking fire. Anna unloaded the purchases on the table that was draped with a torn cover. Mrs Noakes felt over them, and Anna saw that her sight was bad.

The old woman picked up a packet of cigarettes, smelt it and said, 'That's good of you dear. I light up and put it in her mouth. A fag keeps you going.'

Anna said, 'I've been thinking about you. I'd better ring a hospital.'

'No dear. We don't want no orspital.'

'Look. It's too much of a strain on you.'

A tear from under the glasses stole down Mrs Noakes's cheek. 'I got a strained shoulder with all that lifting.'

'Well then . . . You don't want to get ill yourself.'

Mrs Noakes had lighted a cigarette with a bit of paper. The smell a little disguised the smell of dirt, but the figure in the chair began a long rasping cough. Anna said with the authority of youth, 'You can't go on like this.'

But it took ten minutes of argument before Mrs Noakes would give way. It seemed that she, like Miss Sparrow, had seen better times and she had kept an independent spirit. Hospital represented some threat and a loss of liberty. However Anna said, not very hopefully, that medical treatment might make Miss Sparrow more able to look after herself. 'I'd go to a doctor, but I'm new to London and don't know one. The hospital could at least find a doctor for you.'

Mrs Noakes gave way in the end. She was, Anna felt, near breaking point. 'OK dear. I suppose they could come and look at her.'

Anna's flat, still sparsely furnished, seemed incredibly clean and comfortable when she returned. She found the nearest hospital from the telephone book and rang up. It was Saturday evening, and some departments were closed, and Anna had a long series of conversations and was switched about. Finally she grew impatient and said, 'The woman may die in the night for all I know,' and then at last an official listened and said, 'We'll send somebody round.'

The next day Anna telephoned again. Miss Louise Sparrow had been taken into a ward.

Three evenings later Anna walked down the long ward. It was warm after the chilly autumn evening, and seemed a world on its own. In the streets outside people moved about governed by time, but here, behind the swing doors, there seemed no time, and nothing seemed to move.

It was an old-fashioned building which once had been an infirmary, and the long ward seemed to stretch to infinity. On each side was a line of high beds with toothless vacant faces on pillows. Some stared as Anna went by; others had closed eyes. They were like waxworks.

Anna with a bunch of chrysanthemums went right to the end and came back. She could not see Miss Sparrow. She met a young nurse going up and down, straightening a blanket here and lifting a head on to a pillow there. Anna said, 'A Miss Sparrow isn't here, is she?', and the girl led her to a bed where one of the waxworks had closed eyes. But it did not look in the least like the Miss Sparrow of the chair. It had clean silvery hair combed back and clean ivory cheeks with a faint flush. The crabbed veined hands on the coverlet were also clean with white nails.

'Can this be Miss Sparrow?' Anna asked the young nurse.

'She's had a bath,' the girl said, and added quite kindly, 'It's a bit of a shock to some of them when they come in.'

If Miss Sparrow was clean she was also extinguished. Before, she had made sounds which her friend understood. Now she did not open her eyes. 'Miss Sparrow,' Anna said several times. But there was no response. The nurse spoke as if the figure could not hear. 'She's tired, I expect. It's a long day for them.'

The nurse took the flowers and said obligingly, 'I'll get a vase and put it on her locker.' Anna stood for a few minutes by the bed, and one or two old faces were turned to watch. But Miss Sparrow never opened her eyes. In the end Anna turned away and went between the lines of beds and out at the swing door.

She came on another nurse talking to a tall man, but she hardly noticed them. She wanted to get away. Her appearance however interrupted their conversation, and the nurse turned to go saying, 'We're sorry about it. You should have been told.' She had a slight air of deference as if the man were someone in authority. He said, 'Thanks. Her family will make arrangements, I suppose.'

Anna went down the stairs, and he followed. She was tired and stumbled at the bottom, and he caught at her arm. She thanked him, and he asked with that small air of authority, 'Have you found the patient you wanted?'

She told him that she had. 'But that old women's ward is pretty depressing.'

He said that it was an old-fashioned hospital and arrangements would be different in a new building. Anna heard a slight trace of Midland accent in his voice, and asked, 'Do you come from anywhere near Birmingham?'

'I used to, but not now. I haven't been back for years.'

'It's my home town,' she said, but she caught some embarrassment in his voice and asked no more. As he opened the door for her she glanced up at him. He had strong features, a jutting chin and looked, she thought, like some Roman legionary. He must be in his thirties.

Outside rain poured down. She opened her umbrella and was leaving him when he asked, 'Have you far to go?' She said, 'Only to Vizor Street,' and he said, 'Five minutes from my surgery.' She had suspected that he was a doctor.

He offered her a lift, of course. She was depressed and did not want to talk but she could not refuse. She waited in the hospital doorway while he fetched the car, and said as they drove away, 'I suppose you have a lot of old patients.'

'Of course. The woman I went to see this evening has died.'

'You must see some awful things.'

Tristram Forrest might have said something memorable about the human condition, but this man only said, 'I suppose so.' She judged him to be matter-of-fact, reserved and perhaps not very clever. Certainly he had not Tristram's gift of words.

He took her straight to her flat, and she thanked him and ran to her door. The rain was too heavy for much conversation, but he did say as she opened her door and switched on the light, 'I hope we shall meet again.'

Anna had known that Tristram would come back, and he came a week after their first meeting. As she sat in her office she had had a telephone call and had known in some secret way that it was he. He asked if he might call that afternoon. Anybody less polite, she thought, would have just walked in.

When he came she still played what seemed a game of formality. She looked gravely at the pieces that he had brought in as he stood silent by the window. She picked out one account of Paris trees, and again was charmed by the vivid description of the Champs Elisées, but she only said, 'Add a bit about the tourist season, and they might consider it for the spring. I'll send it if you like.'

He turned back from the window. 'I wonder what St Paul would have made of Fleet Street.' These odd remarks, she was to find, were typical.

Their intimacy grew quite naturally. He came to the office at five o'clock, and she said on the third occasion, 'I've finished for the day. I'd like to know more about France. Shall we have a coffee?'

They went out together and sat over the coffee for an hour, and she learnt a little about him. She already knew that he lived at Hampstead. Now she heard that he had joined his father, who had retired as a civil servant from the Ministry of Education. Two old aunts 'hovered' near. Tristram had been at the Sorbonne for three years and now vaguely thought of teaching but he was chiefly interested in writing. 'Nothing, I expect, that would be marketable,' he said. 'Nothing about crime. I prefer rainbows.' Anna thought that this was a good summing up of his character.

On her side she wanted to confide in him; to make her life open to him. She talked of her mother who had always been a reformer, acted as welfare officer in the family factory and read Victorian literature. Dad managed the firm, never read a book for pleasure but was a wizard with all kinds of apparatus and machinery. Then there was Hughie, her younger brother. 'I helped to look after him as my mother was so busy. He's like Dad, keen on gadgets, but he's a baby still though he is seventeen.'

She thought that it sounded a very bourgeois household, but Tristram seemed impressed with Dad. 'Where did the human race get the ability to mend light switches? I couldn't service a bathroom-tap.'

The Staffordshire office agreed to take Tristram's Paris article, though the assistant editor wrote that it would have to be cut a little. Anna marvelled that he made no comment on the charm of the style. Tristram himself seemed surprised at the acceptance. 'Very odd,' he said, 'to be part of a Staffordshire daily. It's a development I should never have expected.'

'You'll have to go on now,' Anna said. 'You could do quite well with articles on France.'

He looked at her and said, 'Is it worth it?' He seemed to care not at all about money or a career. He was an only child, and Anna imagined that his father financed him.

In a few weeks they were meeting regularly, and, though they still talked of his writing and Anna was suggesting papers that he might try, she somehow stepped down from being an adviser and spread out her life for his judgment. She told him of the events she had attended and the people she had met, and he listened in his usual interested way, sometimes making amused comments. 'Emphasis on snippets,' he said, and she defended herself. 'I know, but I've got to earn a living.'

In those early days Anna was happy as she had never been before. One man in her office called her 'Little Miss Bright-Face'. Tristram said almost nothing about himself, but he soon seemed to take it for granted that they should meet weekly. Sometimes he hurt her a little by going off in a detached way with only a brief goodbye, but she could always reflect that she would see him the next week.

He seemed to have many friends both in England and France, and on one occasion she watched how his charm worked. He was away for many week-ends, but one Saturday afternoon she invited him to her flat to advise on pictures. He showed then that he had a good knowledge of painting. The flat, above a stationer's shop, looked out on to a small side street, and he said that she should have landscapes to make it less urban. Some Impressionist painting was obvious. What about a poppy field by Renoir or early spring blossom by Sisley? Constable too – some view of Salisbury perhaps.

Anna said, 'Come to some picture shops with me and help me to choose.' It was part of her attempt to draw him into her life, and he made her happy by saying, 'I've not much judgment, but if you like.' After tea she walked out with him to the Underground at Waterloo, and they passed the red brick surgery at the corner that belonged to the doctor whom she had seen at the hospital. Then they met him.

The tall figure came apparently from putting his car away at the back. He saw Anna and said good evening. She answered and passed by, but Tristram stopped, looked up at the door-bells and said, 'Are you a doctor?'

'A kind of one,' the tall figure said, pausing at the top of the steps.

Tristram said, 'Does your profession make you think a lot about death?'

'On the contrary. We do our best to ignore it.'

'Yet it does happen.'

'Of course it does.'

'It must be a privilege to be at so many death-beds,' Tristram said.

The doctor lingered and said, 'An odd conversation for a Saturday evening.' He looked across to where Anna stood. 'Would you both like to come in for some coffee?'

Anna With Tristram

Tristram said, 'I'd like to ask you more, but I've got to get back to Hampstead. Thanks for talking.' He waved and walked on to Anna, and the doctor opened his door and went in. Tristram said casually, 'An amiable man. What's he called?'

'Dr Gregg, I think. What made you ask all those questions about death?'

'I suppose because it's important,' he said still casually.

They went on to the station talking about pictures. Anna thought afterwards how entertaining he made the world. One never knew what he would say to people.

Anna sometimes thought that Tristram unconsciously mirrored situations ahead. He had asked the doctor about death, and the next morning she had a call from the hospital to say that Miss Louise Sparrow had died. Miss Sparrow had been in the hospital less than a month. Anna had visited her once more, but there was no point because the waxen figure on the high pillows had not recognised her.

The sister who announced the death said, 'She doesn't seem to have any relations that we can contact. The cremation is on Thursday. We shall send somebody along, but I don't suppose that anybody else will be there.'

There is no point, of course, in attending cremations. It is only the clearing up after the event. But Anna, with a vision of a bare coffin and a service read to nobody, took time off on the Thursday morning and went to look for the crematorium. She said to Tristram afterwards that in a way she felt guilty, for if she had not arranged for Miss Sparrow to go to hospital she might still be sitting in that ghastly chair. He said, 'People think there is a choice when really there isn't any. You couldn't help ringing up the hospital.'

But on that dim morning in early December she was questioning her reputation of rushing to get things done. Tristram, who made her so happy, never seemed to interfere with anything. But anyhow there was no going back. Miss Sparrow was dead.

In the last few days Anna had been going round the large shops and writing of Christmas decorations for her London Letter. Now, as she turned up the narrow side street and saw a gleam of grass and heavy wet bushes, she had a sense of relief. Death, she thought, always turns us back to the green world.

Behind the frame of dark leaves and branches was the low red building of the crematorium. By it, at the end of the path, stood two figures – a neat young nurse, the one that Anna had seen going round the ward, and a small figure in rusty black, Mrs Dot Noakes, the friend. She carried two roses.

Anna waited beside them making, as one does on such occasions, irrelevant remarks about the weather. Mrs Noakes said to her, 'I thought you might have looked in on me, dear.'

The coffin arrived and the old woman stumbled forward with her roses. Anna saw that she was much blinder than she had suspected. Then the young nurse took Mrs Noakes's arm to lead her into the chapel. There were only the three of them for the service, read hurriedly by a red-faced parson. Mrs Noakes took off her glasses and wiped her eyes several times, but the reading took only ten minutes and then the curtains were drawn on Miss Sparrow. As they emerged another party was waiting.

The nurse took Mrs Noakes's arm again to keep her off the grass. The old woman said, 'Sorry dear. Things are a bit blurry.'

'How did you manage to get here?'

'I been here before for my hubby and brother-in-law.'

'Who's your doctor?'

'I ain't got no doctor, dear.'

The nurse said to Anna, 'I'd better see her home. But she'll have to have a doctor.'

The fighting spirit seemed to have gone out of Mrs Noakes. She said, 'I don't know I'm sure.'

'We'll arrange it for you.' She was a kind young girl. 'There's a Doctor Gregg who lives near you.'

They parted at the gate, and Mrs Noakes said to Anna, 'It's lonely without Lou,' and Anna, remembering that the old woman was almost helpless in the London streets, said, 'I'll come to see you at the week-end.'

Laurence Gregg had stopped a moment to watch the couple walk away under the lamplight. The light fell on the girl's fair hair and reminded him of the few happy months that he had had in childhood. The face was different, of course, but he thought back to the time when he was sitting in the garden and playing Halma with the child next door.

There was no surgery on a Saturday evening. He would have supper, glance through a pile of medical advertisements that had come in during the week, look at the news on television and do some reading. In a way he would relish the free evening, but there would be nobody to talk to except old Jack, the seaman who occupied the top rooms in the house and waited on him. The next day he might walk by the river for exercise and perhaps drive Jack to the National Maritime Museum. Then the week of coughs and running noses would begin again. He was staying in town at Christmas to do duty for doctors who wanted to get away. He would have nobody much to speak to except a possible patient or two and old Jack; but he was used to a solitary life.

Old Jack came in to ask if he was ready for supper. He said, 'When you like,' and got into his slippers. But he did not read the circulars. He was remembering the light on the fair head, and he realised that, as he drove through the streets in the week, he had looked out for the girl. He had seen her once or twice, but she had been alone.

More than twenty years before he had had the other fair-haired girl as a companion. He had been an only child and she was the youngest in her family. For two years they had played and cycled among the trees of Solihull, but then it came to an abrupt end.

He had been used to listening to his parents' quarrels. Now his mother who had been away a good deal – 'staying with friends', his father said – disappeared. The housekeeper said she had gone to Canada and was not coming back. He had not liked her much. She had seemed too busy to take a great deal of notice of him, and she had a shrill voice when she was quarrelling with his father. But he was ashamed at her departure and did not tell the boys at school. Then the housekeeper said that his parents were getting divorced and she would marry again and stay in Canada. She sent him a card for his birthday, but then the war broke out and he heard no more. He did not much mind.

The family home had been sold and the fair little girl had disappeared. Laurence's father took a flat nearer the centre of Birmingham, which was a pity in view of the air-raids that were to come, but Laurence was sent away to boarding school in Gloucestershire. In spite of the upset of war, the boys of the school remained conventional with family cars and pretty sisters and Laurence kept quiet about his family background. He became known as 'the secret agent', and what friends he had were among the humbler and less remarked boys. While the raids were on in the Midlands his father arranged for him to stay on at school in the holidays with one or two other boys. There was a humorist among them who made Laurence a target for his wit, and the holidays were worse than the terms.

When Laurence began to go home again at the end of the war he hardly knew his father. The elder Gregg had been in one of the Ministries and had seemed to have become gentler in his manners and was not unfriendly. Laurence was now in his teens, and in spite of his school isolation was doing well at lessons. He pleased his father by saying that he would like to be a doctor. Some distant older cousin had been a consultant, and that was the only family thing of which the boy could be proud.

In those years after the war Laurence grew tall but remained silent, and now at school the younger boys were afraid of him. In the holidays his father was out a great deal rebuilding his travel business and attending dinners and social engagements. Laurence, though without friends, did not go after girls, as the quarrels between his parents had sickened him. He tried drinking at pubs and came home fuddled once or twice to be sent to bed by the housekeeper. But then he grew tired of the lights and chatter of public houses and stayed at home with books and television.

His father offered him training in Birmingham or London. He chose London to get away from home. His father seemed relieved, and life became better for Laurence. With the mixed students, many from overseas, it did not matter that one's parents were divorced, and it was the custom to laugh at one's family. Laurence made some good friends, though among the men not women, and life was easier when he went home. His father seemed to take some pride in him and introduced him at his club. Laurence heard people congratulating the elder Gregg on his 'good serious boy'.

But then the situation changed again. Laurence had met Daphne once or twice at the flat – a secretary with swept-back hair and eye-shadow and the habit of laughing a great deal and stroking his father's sleeve. Now his father wrote cordially that he hoped Laurence would approve. He was going to marry Daphne next month. It would be a register-office affair but there would be a reception and he hoped Laurence would come.

Laurence went and found the hotel room full of his father's business friends and Daphne's secretary acquaintances. There was much drinking and joking and the only person Laurence enjoyed talking to was a night watchman who entertained him with stories of bombs on Birmingham. It was perhaps from that moment that Laurence decided to become a general practitioner in an urban area and not to try for the heights of the profession.

For some months both his father and Daphne seemed to want to see him. They had moved into an expensive new house, and the old housekeeper left. Daphne installed a smart woman housekeeper and a girl to do the housework, with a man when they entertained, which was frequently. Laurence did not much like the company who drank a great deal and told smutty stories. But he went back because he seemed wanted, and his father seemed satisfied.

But then there came a development that perplexed him. Daphne had always allowed herself to be kissed by stout middle-aged businessmen, and the elder Gregg had not seemed to notice. But now Daphne appeared to be trying to attract himself, Laurence. She criticised his clothes, said his hair needed cutting, and gave him presents of socks and ties. She played the affectionate relation, laughing and saying that he was working too hard; that he needed more female society.

Again his father did not seem to notice, but Laurence tried not to be alone with her. His avoidance seemed to stimulate her further. She wrote him several small scented notes asking him to come and 'liven us up'. Laurence who, as far as he knew, had never livened anyone, came because he was asked, and Daphne put a hand on his shoulder and said he smelt of disinfectant. But still his father did not seem aware of her advances.

Her chase came to a dramatic end. One evening the couple returned from a dinner party, the older Gregg flushed and stumbling a little. He disappeared upstairs, but Daphne, all fur and diamonds, danced humming about the room where Laurence was reading. She unpinned a spray of carnations and came and leaned over the back of his chair, putting her arms round his shoulders and holding the flowers to his nose. 'Diddums smell,' she said. He moved to get up, but she pressed him down and laughed, and at that moment his father returned.

How much he had seen of Daphne's flirtations Laurence did not know. But he did not ignore this. He had suffered with his previous wife, and his fury seemed the greater. He glared at Laurence and said, 'You unspeakable swine.' Daphne laughed and danced out of the room, and the two Greggs were left, both with bitter memories.

Laurence made no excuses. He was not used to such situations, and he could not poison the marriage further by accusing Daphne. His father, red in the face, shouted, 'Get out of here.' It was eleven at night, but he followed Laurence upstairs and stood at the door while Laurence packed his bag. Laurence finished, put on his coat and went downstairs, his father following. The elder Gregg opened the front door and Laurence went out. The door was slammed behind him, and he spent the night at a hotel, and then returned to London.

In two days he received a typewritten letter telling him never to return. His father died a year later, and Daphne inherited the family property. Laurence heard from the previous housekeeper that she, Daphne, married again after thirteen months. He had not been back to the Midlands since. They had become a place to be avoided.

Life should have been pleasant for the four-year-old Irene Meredith. Her parents, Helena and Jos, regarded her as a great treasure, and they got on well together. Her old uncle Edward Carey showed her pictures of flowers in his books, and Millie in the kitchen had two good old cats. Benedict, Irene's grown-up brother at Cambridge, was very tall and surprising, and the whole house seemed to be excited when he arrived back. Then there was Rose who had gone to Yorkshire but always brought presents when she came back. Jenny Owen, the big girl who played with Irene and loved Benedict, told stories of magic. Behind the house the gardens stretched down to the orchard and what seemed almost the end of the world, and there were glass-houses with flowers above Irene's head and tomato plants with their strange scent and green and red fruit that came, it seemed, out of nowhere.

But in fact Irene's life was often hell. It was poisoned by the creatures in the two bedrooms. When Benedict was away she slept in his room on the first landing, and she could see a glow of light and could hear voices from below. But even then there were terrors in that room. A bookcase had a sharp edge which became the face of a wicked old man and the curtains in summer waved to and fro as if ghosts were in them. There was sometimes a wolf under the bed. Irene knew that he was there though he kept deadly quiet.

But in the upper room where she went when Benedict was at home it was worse. Millie slept up there and Rose had a room. But

Anna With Tristram

Millie was in the kitchen and Rose had gone to Yorkshire and Irene was all alone. When she went to bed a low light would be left on the landing, but all human comfort was far away. In that high room there were many creatures. There was a cupboard with a shut door, and behind the door was a witch who tied people up. The dressing-table had a mirror which vaguely reflected the light, and an oily snake with burning eyes coiled round in the glass and might come out at any moment and bite you with its poisoned teeth. Most terrible was a white figure that stood motionless upright in a corner. It was a dead frozen man who could not move or speak but was crying all the time with ice tears that cracked on the floor.

Irene told almost no-one about these terrors, and often forgot them in the day. But, when her mother took her up for a bath and an evening read, the pleasure was mixed with awful fear. She would try to keep Helena there by saying that she was thirsty or needed her teddy-bear, but then her father would come up to say goodnight, and the two would go down together, and their voices would die away and the terrors would begin.

The only person who knew anything about them was Jenny, the big girl of fourteen who came to play with Irene and lingered when Benedict was about. Jenny said that children could see things that grown-ups couldn't. The best thing to do was to pull the covers over your head and keep saying 'Matthew, Mark, Luke and John' who were saints and would protect you. Irene found that this did help you to go to sleep.

But Jenny had stories of her own which made the fears worse. Irene thought that Jenny did not mean to frighten her. She was just a wonderful story-teller. She said that there were tigers in the woods on Clissold Hill, and if you went there at night you would see their eyes gleaming. In a field by the Worcester road were plants with flowers like mauve tongues, and if you touched one you dropped down dead. But worst was the Iron House near the churchyard. A farmer had once kept stores there, but now it was empty with rust on its corrugated iron roof. It stood behind a line of elder bushes so that you did not see it properly, and so it was a good meeting place for the ghosts of dead people in the churchyard next door. Irene had better not go near it.

Jenny had stories too about the eight boys at Meadow Grange, the big house near The Hollies, Irene's home. Long ago Rose, who worked for the social services, had suggested that it might be a home for delicate or handicapped boys, and now they were sent out to improve their health in the country. The field behind belonged to Uncle Edward, who had let the boys have a bit of land at the top for games. Jenny's old pony Frost had lived in the field till he died, and Jenny had permission to go there still to pick wild flowers in the hedges. So she talked to the boys sometimes, and she told Irene stories about them. One boy had been so delicate when he was born that he had to be wrapped in cotton wool for six months, and the father of another one was a dwarf only two feet high.

The oldest boy, now about fourteen, was called Steve Hitchen, but Jenny called him Crabby. This was because of his strange left hand which had two middle fingers missing. Crabby said that this was through a farm accident, but Jenny said he was making this up. He was really the son of a crab and a lady. He had been born in the middle of England, but he was always trying to get back to the sea, and when he got there he might turn into an enormous real crab. They met him sometimes when Jenny took Irene down to the village shop kept by her father. He seemed quite an ordinary rough boy, except for his strange hand, and he had freckles and thick untidy hair. Jenny, who was clever at school, would greet him in a superior way and ask him if he could do fractions or knew where Tokyo was. He always replied, 'You're a funny girl.'

Jenny behaved very differently to Irene's big brother Benedict. She gazed at him with wide eyes and hardly said a word. Benedict was kind to Irene, running about the garden with her on his back and puffing and saying, 'I am the west wind.' But if Jenny came to watch he would take no notice of her, or, if Jenny was looking at a book with Uncle Edward, Benedict would come in and hold a conversation over her head. But all his rudeness seemed to make Jenny dote on him more than ever.

Christmas was coming now, and Jenny's father, who stocked Christmas cards, had given her a box so that she could choose what she wanted for her friends. Irene was with her as she dived into the charming stack of pictures. Jenny was quite careless when she put some aside for school friends, but then she said, 'The best shall go to your family.' She picked out the pretty picture of a round tree in a pot, and said, 'I'll give this to Benedict. He likes verses.'

Benedict came home for Christmas, and they were all sitting at tea when Jenny came up in the dark on Christmas Eve. Millie let her in, and she went silently round the backs of their chairs slipping cards in their places. Jenny had taken care over those cards. Irene herself had a fairy on a Christmas tree which she had not seen before. Uncle

Edward had a robin on a snowy spade, and Rose, who was down from Yorkshire, had a manger with a baby because she was kind. Irene's parents had a big book with a lighted candle, and Benedict had the pretty round tree in a pot with a bird and verses that Jenny had shown to Irene. The company opened the cards, showed one another and said 'What a good idea' – all except Benedict. He put his hand to his head and pretended to be in despair. 'Not *another* partridge in a pear tree,' he said and flicked the card across the table to Jos. Helena said sharply, 'Benedict mind your manners.' But Jenny had gone away silently.

It was after Christmas that Anna began to visit Mrs Noakes weekly. The dirty old house by the arch had changed a little. Another tenant was in Miss Sparrow's old room and the door was shut. Mrs Noakes said that the railway, which owned the property, had sent in two men to clear the room, but they said there was nothing there worth twopence. The new tenant was lah-di-dah, had some man in attendance and didn't even say good-morning. 'Lou was a trouble but she was a bit of company,' Mrs Noakes said.

Mrs Noakes did her best to entertain Anna. She tidied the room and put out bright-coloured fancy cakes that the kid down the street had bought. She put cups on a tin tray and poured out strong tea, and she always greeted Anna in the same way. 'Come in, dear. I ain't had a chat all day.'

The chat came nearly all from her. It was mainly about the district before the war – the people of the noisy New Cut, and pubs and outings to the races. Mrs Noakes's father had come of an Italian family, and he sold ice-cream in summer and hot chestnuts and pies in winter. Her mother's family had had a flower stall. Whether her parents were married Mrs Noakes did not say, but she was the youngest of a large family which drifted away so that she hardly knew the older ones. 'I was good-looking in them days, dear, and I left off my glasses and dressed up fine and I had no end of young men.' She became a barmaid and, tired of poverty, eventually married the publican.

But her chief story, repeated many times, was of 'my Ted'. Many young men came into the pub for the sake of Dot Noakes. 'I knew how to handle them lot, dear.' But Ted was different. He was a real gentleman and worked at some Government office. He had travelled a great deal, and he spoke in a gentleman's way. He had a beautiful face, like a choirboy's and he smoked only Turkish cigarettes. 'He would come and talk to me but always very respectful,' and he would tell Dot about the places he had seen, the lovely women he had met and the rich people of the 'Riveera'. 'But – you wouldn't think it now dear – but he said I was as pretty as any of them.'

She had known him only a year. Then he told her that his office was moving him, and he came to say goodbye. 'I cried all that evening, but I told my hubby I had a cold.'

However that was not quite the end. The war came and the 'hubby' was called up and Dot got a good job in a canteen. In the raids she spent the night in air-raid shelters, but one night she wanted some cigarettes and came out to fetch them from her room. A raid was on, and suddenly a building was hit and she was knocked sideways. She found herself lying on the pavement and somebody leaning over her, 'and, blow me, if it wasn't my Ted. He must have been a warden or something.' He said, 'I never kissed you before, but I'll kiss you now,' and he bent and gave her a long kiss, but then the ambulance came, and she was taken to hospital with a broken arm. She had not seen him since, but she wished – oh how she wished – that she knew where he was.

Anna never knew how much of this story was true. At any rate it gave Mrs Noakes great pleasure in remembering it.

Anna brought in stores, and they talked comfortably for an hour. Once or twice it was of 'that doctor' that the hospital had sent. 'He said as how he lived near you, dear – a gentlemanly man, and he gave me a good examination. I told him I could do with some new glasses as I don't see as well as I did.'

'And what did he say?'

'Said as he'd come again for a talk. I hope he'll come soon. Make a break in the day.'

Anna also hoped that he would come soon, for she was worried about Mrs Noakes's safety. The old woman had an open fire with a very small grate, and sometimes hot cinders fell on to the wooden floor. Mrs Noakes did not seem aware of them till she smelt the burning smell and got up and with her old crooked poker tried to scrape them back to the small hearth of cracked tiles. The fire itself was small and the floor-boards old and coated with dirt; so there was probably little risk. But one could never be sure.

Anna's intervention with Miss Sparrow had led to her, Miss

Sparrow's, death in hospital. It was clear that well-intentioned deeds are not always successful. All the same Anna was her mother's child, and if there was something to be done she had to do it. She said, 'I think I'd better ring up the doctor,' and went home and telephoned.

She knew little of Dr Gregg except that he seemed to admire her and she did not want his admiration. He seemed solitary, reserved and perhaps dull, though when Tristram had gone back to speak to him he had been friendly. But Tristram, she thought, always charmed people.

Dr Gregg had one fervent admirer – old Jack who lived at the top of the surgery. Anna often saw Jack about with his wizened eagle face, short cropped white hair and incessant conversation. Somebody had told her that the doctor had rescued him from a doss-house, and now he acted as a cook assistant, preparing meals and answering the telephone when the doctor was out. He had two main topics for his flow of talk – his experiences in the war and the doctor, in whom he seemed to have an almost fatherly pride. The doctor, he said, could have been a 'top man', but preferred to be a G.P. among the poor old folk of south London.

At any rate the doctor had called promptly on Mrs Noakes and she had liked him. And when Anna spoke to him that evening, though it was Saturday, he immediately invited her to the surgery for a discussion.

She went round at about seven. It was a cold evening, but the door seemed to have been left open for her, and she rang and walked in. She found the waiting-room and receptionist's office empty, and the nineteenth-century building with high ceilings gave an impression of gloom and chill. But the doctor opened the door of his consulting room and said, 'It's good of you to come.' He had been reading by a small gas fire, but he turned it up and offered coffee.

Anna refused. She did not know him well and was a little afraid of him. 'I won't stay. I've all my week-end housework to do.'

As it was, however, she stayed nearly an hour arguing over Mrs Noakes. Sometimes, she thought afterwards, she had been too emphatic, but then the doctor, in her eyes, was too full of commonsense and balanced judgment, and this fretted her.

She asked about Mrs Noakes's eyes. 'She thinks you might arrange new glasses.' He replied that no new glasses would help. Her eyes had been scarred by measles when she was a child, and she was now over seventy and the sight was just not there. Mrs Noakes had told him that she had been to an 'eye man' years before, and he had said that there was no chance of improvement.

'Haven't things moved at all since then?' Anna asked.

'Not in this case,' he said calmly, and this irritated her. She tried to spur him on by describing the fire risks in that isolated ancient room. He listened patiently as no doubt he listened to talkative patients, and then said, 'I have already found her a place in a home.'

'You have? Why didn't you say? Will she be happy there?'

He said in his judicial way, 'It's the best that I can do. I'm doctor at the Garden Home and so the matron's stretching a point to take Mrs Noakes. They don't really want a blind resident.'

'But they've agreed, and it's all right.'

'I hope so. The home is rather congested. There are not nearly enough of these homes about, and the council tries to accommodate as many residents as possible.'

Again his calm attitude stung her. She wanted enthusiasm, joy that Mrs Noakes would now be safe.

'Thank goodness,' she said. 'I've been worried.'

But he damped her down again. 'There is a problem.'

'How can there be if they've agreed?'

'But Mrs Noakes hasn't.'

'But surely, if it's a nice place . . .'

'How would you like to leave the home that you've known for twenty years and go and live with strangers?'

Old Jack had told Anna that the doctor was popular because he saw the patients' point of view. But now she said, half-indignantly, 'You seem to keep on making objections.'

He did not hit back; only asked, 'How often do you see Mrs Noakes?'

'I try to see her once a week.'

The doctor said, 'I'm sending her a notification tonight. Can you look in and discuss it with her and persuade her that it's for her own good? She will have to decide soon.'

Anna got up still a little exasperated. 'You make everything seem so difficult.'

'It's no good being romantic about old people's homes,' he said. 'They have many problems.'

'Do you want me to tell Mrs Noakes that?'

'Of course not.'

She said half under her breath, 'Sometimes I'm surprised that you official people get anything done.'

He heard and said stiffly as he saw her out, 'I think you lack experience, Miss Dean.'

She was ashamed afterwards and for that reason was especially fervent in her talks with Mrs Noakes. She described the Garden Home as a place in which kind people would fulfil every need. Mrs Noakes resisted for a time, but Anna paid several visits and the weather was bitterly cold and Mrs Noakes's room arctic. In the end she said that she would 'try for a bit', and Anna did not enlighten her that the move would be permanent.

She had succeeded, but she kept the impression that she might have been rude to the doctor. Instead of telephoning she wrote that Mrs Noakes had agreed to move, and added, 'Forgive me if I argued too much the other night. I'd had a long day.'

He sent a brief note back saying that Mrs Noakes was being moved in a few days. He ignored her apology.

Anne and Tristram were watching a French film. It was a wet Saturday afternoon, and he had not gone into the country as he generally seemed to do. This was the first time that they had been to the cinema together, and she glanced sideways at him once or twice. She had to concentrate to follow the language, but he, being used to French, sat back with his long fingers folded in his lap. She felt the intense pleasure of having him beside her, and yet as he sat there he seemed detached and inaccessible.

The lights went up, and she realised why she felt vaguely disappointed. A couple sat in front of them, the woman elegant, buxom and middle-aged, and the man sharp-faced and older. The two had been holding hands, and now, slowly, unwillingly, the two hands drew apart, the man giving a final squeeze to the plump fingers with their long red nails.

It happened everywhere of course. But it had not happened with Tristram. He had sat quite detached. Anna, as a student has discussed love many times, but she had been one of a hard-working group which disapproved of the houris, the much bedecked girls who always attracted crowds of noisy young men. She had had men friends and felt the warmth of an arm round her shoulders, but there had been no serious entanglements. She had vaguely thought that she was too young for marriage which might or might not come later. Meanwhile she had many other things to do.

But now, suddenly, everything was different. There was no question of waiting. Love was here. It had become more important than anything else and she had wanted him to stretch out his hand. But he had sat almost as if he were unaware of her.

She followed him closely as they emerged. If he had said 'Come home to tea' she would have been delighted to travel all the way to Hampstead. But he did not, and she feared a refusal if she asked him to her flat. So they drifted into the inevitable café.

Inside was a Saturday crowd, and they had to share a table. Opposite them were a youngish man and woman who were having a quarrel. They lowered their voices only a little when Anna and Tristram sat down. The man had a habit of saying 'Sez-you' and the woman kept balling her fist and rapping the table.

She was complaining of his lateness at their meetings. 'You've no sense of time, and you don't care who you keep waiting.' He said, 'Nag. Nag. Nag,' and she banged with her fist and said, 'All right, if that's your attitude. This will be the last time.' He shrugged. 'OK. There are other fish in the pond.' Finally she sprung up and walked out, and he kicked at a chair and strolled after her. Anna was embarrassed, but Tristram watched them with slightly raised eyebrows and a smile.

Anna said when they had gone 'Why do people stay together if they hate one another so much?'

He answered lightly, 'They probably don't hate one another all the time. There's generally a reaction – compliments instead of insults.'

He spoke of people, Anna thought, as if he did not belong to them. She still knew little about him. She asked a personal question. 'Have you ever hated anyone?'

He slipped away from a personal answer. 'Hatred covers a lot of different feelings.'

'No, but don't *you* ever quarrel with anyone?'

He muttered under his breath with a bitterness she did not understand, 'I'm not one to get involved.'

She said, voicing a disappointment that was already darkening her happiness, 'I wish you'd tell me more about yourself.'

'Oh dear,' he said with a sigh, and she was frightened that she was pestering him too much. She was slave to every expression on that handsome face, and murmured, 'Sorry. I'm being boring.'

He did not answer, and she began to talk rapidly about her own affairs. He listened as usual with interest and asked questions, and it seemed that her complaint had been covered up. But he said at the end, 'You mustn't expect too much of me, Anna.' And then came the dreaded, 'I must go.'

They walked to the Underground and then stood on the escalator, one behind the other. She felt his nearness and yet knew that she would spend the rest of the evening depressed because he so much held himself apart.

At the bottom of the stairs she said, 'When?' and he replied, 'Thursday, I suppose. Usual place.' And then they went their separate ways.

The Oxford-Cambridge Boat Race had finished with the usual Cambridge victory. Dr Gregg and old Jack, standing on the towpath, had not taken sides. The old sailor had wanted to see the craft on the river, and the doctor had brought him because he liked Jack to be amused.

Since his retirement Jack had not had much of a life. Like many old sailors he was solitary, never having married. He had had no home to return to and had settled for a few months at Portsmouth and there grown interested in model-making. But he had not found the light job that he wanted and so, in winter, had moved to London. In cheap lodgings he had developed pneumonia, and Dr Gregg had been called in. Jack needed shelter, and the doctor had the big house at the corner, and so he had invited the old sailor to occupy two rooms temporarily. He had bought some cheap furniture for him and the old man had settled down, and it soon had become obvious that he would stay. He was always cheerful and he had taken on shopping and cooking and, when necessary, answering the telephone. The two suited one another, the doctor being silent and Jack garrulous.

All that morning on the towpath Jack had been chatting to the crowd. He would turn to a stranger standing by him and say without introduction, 'Were you ever in an open boat on the Atlantic in December?' Some people would turn away or stare in front of them without answering, but the towpath crowds wanted entertainment and until the actual race Jack had had a small group round him while he discoursed on submarine attacks, convoys, disasters and rescues. People commented, 'You're lucky to be here' or 'We didn't know at the time, did we?'

The doctor stood silent, watching Jack. Two young men at the edge of the group caught his attention. One was unusual with dark eyes, a long face and a frizz of light brown hair. The other looked typically English, fair and blue-eyed. The doctor heard one of them say something that sounded like Latin, and the fair one replying, 'It's no good. I'm forgetting it all except for the parts of the body.' Could he be a medical student?

The race began, and there was the usual shouting with crowds running along the towpath. As usual it was over in a remarkably short time, and the crowd, who had waited for hours, began to thin. But Jack lingered watching the boats, and the two young men stood laughing together over some private conversation.

Then a group of rowdy boys came charging by, waving bottles and shouting. They narrowly missed the doctor and Jack but collided with the two young men. One of the two went down, but the group charged on oblivious.

It was the fair youth who was on the ground. The other pulled him up, but he groaned and stood on one leg. 'Hell. They've broken my ankle.' He was grimacing with pain, but the other said desperately, 'We'll have to get back somehow.' The towpath by now was nearly empty.

Laurence said, 'I'm a doctor. Can I help?' The injured one answered politely, 'Thank you very much,' but his friend seemed surprised. '*Another* doctor?'

The fair boy tried to put his foot to the ground and groaned again. Laurence gave the car keys to Jack and said, 'Go and open up and we'll follow.'

As a doctor Laurence was always sure of himself. Now he issued orders. 'We'll get you to my car, and I'll have a look at you.' He and the other boy supported the injured one to the side-street, and Jack had the car doors open. The fair boy plumped down sideways and the other, obviously relieved, said cheerfully, 'He's always having accidents. He fell out of a tree when we were young.'

The doctor got the fair boy's shoe off and looked at the ankle. It was badly swollen, and he asked, 'What are you going to do?'

The two looked at one another blankly. They seemed to the doctor very young. The injured one said, 'We'd better get a taxi,' but there were no taxis about. The solution was obvious. The doctor said,

'You'd better come to my surgery where I can examine you properly, and then you can decide.'

As he drove Laurence heard from their conversation at the back that they came from the Midlands. Warwickshire had been his birthplace and some hidden feeling remained. Also it seemed that the injured one was a medical student. Laurence could not just dismiss them in a taxi. He said to Jack as they stopped at the surgery, 'Can you manage some lunch for them?', and Jack, pleased to be important, ran into the house.

It was an unexpected afternoon. The injured boy hopped with help to the consulting room, and the doctor bandaged the ankle. It had swollen to a great size but, as far as he could tell, it was only bruised. 'You must keep it up while you're here,' Laurence said and provided a stool and a stick. The two had given their names as Alan and Benedict, and it seemed that Benedict, who had been staying on after the end of term at Cambridge, had come to London only for the day to see the boat race.

The boys had a large lunch in the roomy kitchen where the doctor and Jack ate. Jack continued with his war-time experiences in the Merchant Navy. The boys listened attentively to this slice of history they had never known, and at one point Benedict asked, 'Were you ever in the Mediterranean?'

'Yes, and well bombed,' Jack said complacently. 'And then there was Vesuvius erupting.'

'*Vesuvius*,' Benedict cried.

'Yes, and making a fearful dust hundreds of miles away.'

'You were there?'

'Yes mate. I saw it.'

'Marvellous,' the boy cried. 'Can I talk to you?'

Alan explained. 'He's doing a thesis on the Plinys. They're mixed up with Vesuvius.'

'What are Plinys?' Jack asked.

'Oh come now . . .' Benedict said like a schoolmaster, but Alan was quick to temper his arrogance. 'You can't expect everybody to know about your Romans. I don't think any of my lot at St Thomas's . . .'

'St Thomas's,' the doctor repeated.

'It's my hospital.'

'And was mine.'

Benedict said something in Latin, and Alan said laughing, 'You can't stop him.'

After lunch Jack took Benedict upstairs to see photographs of Vesuvius and a book on early Mediterranean craft. Alan stayed downstairs with the doctor and rested his ankle and talked about hospital and discovered mutual acquaintances. He talked too about his home at Ladyhill, and once again the doctor felt the Midlands becoming nearer and less disastrous.

At five Benedict clattered down and said he had a Cambridge train in an hour and a half, and Jack made some tea. Alan's ankle was easier, and the doctor said he would take him to the hospital but first see Benedict off from Liverpool Street Station. The boys were profuse in their thanks, and Alan said, 'I'll have to get your stick back to you somehow.'

'Come and see me again,' the doctor said.

But he felt a little wary of the classical scholar Benedict as he stood with him at the Cambridge train. Benedict himself seemed to think that he might have made an impression of arrogance. 'I know my Latin puts people off. Alan's got crowds of London friends, but I don't know a soul here. I've been told to look up some journalist girl from Birmingham, but haven't had a chance yet.'

'She isn't called Anna Dean?'

'Gracious! Do you know her?'

'Only a little, but she lives near me.'

Benedict made the inevitable remark that it was a small world, and then the train slid away. That evening, when Laurence returned from taking Alan back to the hospital, Jack said, 'You could do with more young company, doctor. Ask them again.'

Benedict, the beautiful Benedict, came home for Easter. He had been a pig about Jenny's Christmas card and ignored her afterwards, but the more he scorned her the more she worshipped him. And now gradually she had evolved a daring plan to soften his heart.

She was going to do something very sensational. Long before, when she was a little girl, she had been lost, and the village had turned out to look for her. Now suppose the little Irene could be lost and Jenny could triumphantly find her. Surely Benedict would look on her more kindly.

Of course she would not harm the little girl, with whom she played almost daily. She would only leave her for an hour or two in a secluded place. She would say that she, Jenny, was coming back, and she *would* come back. She thought that Irene was too young to describe afterwards what actually had happened.

Jenny at the age of fourteen had become vaguely pious with aspirations to help the world and particularly animals. But her love of Benedict was greater than her desire to do good. Love had been there since Benedict and her brother Alan had been friends, and Jenny had been left out. And, though the boys were separated now, one at Cambridge and one in London, they still met in the holidays, and Benedict still treated Jenny as if she were a silly little girl. She would prove that she was not.

On a fine April afternoon Irene was on a seat in the garden with her drawing book and one of Millie's cats. Her parents, she said, were in Birmingham, and Uncle Edward and Millie were looking after her. But Uncle Edward was in a glass-house and Millie was in the kitchen. Benedict, the beautiful Benedict, was upstairs studying.

Jenny, who had come in by the side gate, said, 'Shall we go a little walk?' She often took Irene down to her father's village shop to buy ice-cream or yoghurt.

'I'll tell Millie,' Irene said, but Jenny said, 'I shouldn't bother. We'll only be gone a few minutes – or anyhow not very long,' she corrected herself as she did not want to tell too big lies. The two went out by the side gate, across the front garden and into the sunny road. But Jenny led Irene past the shop, the turning to Jos's pottery, the Ploughman's Arms, the school and the dreadful Iron House behind its elder bushes. Irene said, 'It's a long way. Where are we going?'

'We'll find some celandines for Uncle Edward and we might see the Queen of Spring,' Jenny said, turning up a narrow track to the right. It led to the Shaws, a piece of common land seldom visited at that time of year.

'What's the Queen of Spring?'

'You'll see.'

It was a muddy track, uphill and long, but they came out at last to open grass with scattered trees and bushes. There was a ditch, but no celandines were blooming. They sat on a fallen tree in the sunshine, and Jenny said, 'This is where the Queen of Spring comes at night.'

'But it isn't night,' Irene said.

'It could be. We could build a little house and sleep in it and wake up and peep out and see her flying about.'

'She wouldn't hurt us, would she?' Irene said, remembering her night terrors.

'Of course not. She'd be very lovely, flying about in a green silky dress and touching the trees with her wand.'

'What would my mother say?'

'I know,' Jenny said. 'I'll go and ask her. I'll bring back some tea and blankets and you can start building a house with bits of wood.'

'My mother's gone to Birmingham.'

'She'll be back by now.'

It had been a long walk and Irene was tired. She said, 'All right. Tell my mother about the Queen of Spring,' and Jenny went off down the muddy path to the main road. She felt a little nervous and ashamed but reflected that nothing could harm Irene in the Shaws and she was an obedient child and would not wander away.

For a time Jenny sat in the churchyard. Some of the tombstones were so old and lichened that she could not read the inscriptions, but there were some new white crosses with black lettering, and one said 'Peace, perfect peace'. This was the opposite of what Jenny was feeling at the moment; so she moved away to examine the Iron House at the side of the churchyard. It was a decayed place, shut and silent behind its bushes, though cars were bowling along the main road only a few yards away. Behind the shack was a waste of thistles. Jenny did not believe the stories of ghosts that she had told Irene, but she did not like the place much. She came out and wandered along the road to the bus-stop, which was conveniently past her father's shop so that she would not be seen waiting.

She had timed it well. After ten minutes the bus from Birmingham drew up, and Helena appeared on the step. Jenny was suddenly terrified, but she stuck to her plan. As Helena stepped down Jenny came forward and said, 'Irene's lost.'

The effect was greater than she had anticipated. Helena turned and Jenny would always remember her aghast look. 'Lost? What do you mean?'

'She isn't at home,' Jenny said.

'Where is she?'

Jenny could not say that she did not know. She said, 'They don't know up there.'

Jos had followed Helena out of the bus, and Jenny had an impression of their affection and reliance on one another. She felt ashamed, but she could not say now that it was a joke. Jos took Helena's arm and said 'Steady' and without noticing Jenny any more they strode away up to The Hollies. Jenny let them go and ran back along the road and up the track to the Shaws. She would bring the child back and make up some story. Breathlessly she shouted 'Irene.' But there was no answer. Irene was not there.

It had been a long afternoon for Irene. She had sat on the fallen tree for a time and grown rather cold. Then she began to look for big pieces of wood for building the night house, but she could find only small branches and twigs. She made a pile, however, and sat down again, wishing Jenny would come.

She was beginning to feel sleepy when she saw somebody coming up the muddy path. But it was not Jenny but Crabby, the boy with the funny hand. Irene had never spoken to him directly. She had always been with Jenny when they met him. And there was Jenny's fearful story that he might turn into a crab some day. But now she could not help being glad to see him. He looked good-natured anyway with his thatch of light hair and light eye-lashes.

He came looking along the ditch and suddenly became aware of Irene. He said, 'Crikey. What you doing here?'

'Jenny brought me.' Then Irene thought that the boy might think this odd; so she added. 'We came to look for the Queen of Spring.'

'Is that what she said?'

'Didn't you know,' Irene asked, 'that the Queen of Spring flies round up here?'

Crabby began to laugh. 'She doesn't half tell stories. Where is she?'

'She's gone to get some cake and blankets, and we're going to build a house.'

'Build a nothing,' Crabby said, and Irene, who had had some doubts herself, changed the subject to ask what he was doing there.

Crabby told her that the boys of Meadow Grange had gone down to the shop to buy sweets, but he didn't trouble about such things. At the farm where he had been brought up there had been bee-hives and he had got interested, and he wanted to keep bees himself when he had a good job. Meanwhile he was studying them, and they came out, of course, on spring days. The Shaws were noted for flowers, so he thought he might find early bees up here. But all he had seen were a few bumble bees, and anyhow there weren't any flowers much; only a bit of dead nettle and blackthorn.

'The sun'll soon be setting,' he said. 'I expect the bees will have gone home. You aren't staying here, are you?'

'Jenny told me to stay.'

'I bet she's forgotten what she said.'

It did seem possible. Irene must have waited more than an hour. 'Anyhow,' Crabby said, 'if she's coming we'll meet her.'

The idea of building a house seemed more and more remote. Irene knew that Jenny sometimes made things up. Crabby seemed a very nice boy, and she thought that she did not really want to stay up there all night. 'All right,' she said, and they started off down the path. Crabby went slowly so that she could keep up, and he lifted her over the muddy places. They reached the main road, but there was no sign of Jenny. Crabby said, 'P'raps she's in the churchyard.'

Irene protested, 'She wouldn't go there. There's ghosts in there.'

Crabby said, 'Crazy girl. Don't you listen to her,' and since there was no sign of Jenny the only thing was to go home. They looked in at the shop, but all the boys had gone back to Meadow Grange, and Crabby said that it was tea-time there, and he too must get back. But he took Irene to her own gate and held it open, and she went in and round to the side.

Millie was in the kitchen getting tea. She said, 'Where on earth have you been all the afternoon? You've got twigs in your hair.' There was still no sign of Jenny.

Irene said, 'Jenny wanted some blankets.'

'Jenny can get her own blankets.' Millie sounded rather cross. 'Your sandals are covered with mud, and you're treading it all over my floor. Get them off.'

Then Uncle Edward came in to see if it was tea-time, and he said, 'You've been hiding all the afternoon.' Benedict followed saying, 'What have you been doing going out with that big boy? I saw you from a window.' Irene was just saying that he was a very good big boy and she was helping to get the tea when her parents came running in. They stopped short when they saw her, and Helena rushed at her and picked her up. Helena was breathless, half crying. She said, 'That devil Jenny.'

Irene began to apologise. 'We only wanted to see the Queen of Spring.'

'And who is she?' Jos asked. He was breathless too but not as upset as Helena.

'She has a lovely green dress and she flies round at night with a wand.' Irene saw an amused look on their faces and stopped.

'Where does she fly round?' Jos asked.

'At that place called Shaws.' But Irene did not dare to say anything about the night house.

Jos said, 'What a pity we can't keep our imagination,' but Helena broke in. 'Do you mean to say that you've been all that way with Jenny?'

Then Uncle Edward interrupted. He always stood up for Jenny. 'Irene's back anyhow. Jenny will explain.'

'She'd better,' Helena said, and Benedict, whom Jenny adored so, said in his scornful way, 'That girl should be shut up.'

It was ghastly bad luck, Jenny thought afterwards, that she had not seen Irene and Crabby in the road. She must have been behind the elder bushes looking at the Iron House.

In a way now she was a heroine. She could have gone home and said nothing, but if Irene was really lost she must start a search. She went up to The Hollies to reconnoitre expecting to find confusion, but, as she skirted round the front garden, she saw through the windows the family peacefully at tea, with Irene between her parents and the beautiful Benedict slopping jam on a piece of bread.

Jenny's heart gave a great throb of relief and she was stealing away when Helena saw her. In a minute the front door was flung open and there was Helena glaring like a giantess.

'Jenny, what's all this nonsense?'

Jenny said weakly, 'I only . . .'

'First you tell us that Irene is lost, and then it seems you took her all the way to the Shaws.'

'I-it was only a walk.'

'And left her somewhere, and the boy Steve had to bring her home. If he hadn't been there . . .' Helena gave a little gasp. Jenny had never seen this respected and somewhat remote figure so upset.

Millie had come out and stood, a second vengeful woman, behind Helena. She said, 'Mud all over her and bits of stick in her hair.'

For once Jenny had nothing to say. She backed away down the path, but Helena called after her, 'In future you are not to take Irene out without asking.' The door shut with a bang.

That evening the Owens' telephone rang. Jenny was reading an Enid Blyton in her bedroom, but she could hear her mother's voice saying, 'I'm very sorry.' She stayed quiet, but Mrs Owen came up the stairs. Mrs Owen would not have harmed a fly, but now she looked almost stern. 'Jenny, you've upset Helena. What have you been doing?'

'Only took Irene for a walk.'

'She says you left the child somewhere and the boy Steve had to bring her back.'

Jenny pressed her lips together, and Mrs Owen knew that there was not much chance of getting a confession. In contests with Jenny it was generally Jenny who won. Mrs Owen said. 'Well, you'd better keep away from Irene for a day or two. Anyway you'll be back at school next week.' And she went downstairs leaving Jenny dumb again.

So Jenny did not go up to The Hollies and did not see Benedict, and the days were empty. Her only comfort was talking to Crabby whom she saw when she went wandering in the field behind Meadow Grange. Crabby wanted to know why Jenny had left Irene at the Shaws, but Jenny said it was a secret. They had a good many conversations, and talked about what they would do when they were grown up and free and rich.

Anna did not know what to expect as she went up the path to the Garden Home. She knew nothing about old people's homes but imagined that once you were there you were safe and happy. She had not heard from Mrs Noakes since the old woman had been moved, but then Mrs Noakes was half blind. Anna had rung up to enquire and had been told that Mrs Noakes was 'comfortable' and that she, Anna, could visit at any time. That had given a good impression.

She passed a small plantation of laurels and other bushes and turned towards the house. It was a large Edwardian building in Tudor style, with gables and half-timber work. It had a heavy nail-studded wooden door, and looked as if it might be dark inside. Anna rang.

The door was opened immediately. She was obviously expected, and Mrs Noakes was waiting in the hall. But it was a different Mrs Noakes. Anna saw her before she was aware of Anna, and the effect was devastating.

Miss Sparrow had been cleaned up by the hospital. Mrs Noakes had been both cleaned up and made miserable. The grimed wrinkled face was now pale; the hair was silvery white and the hands with the black nails had become the hands of a lady. But the figure expressed utter misery – drooping mouth, sagging knees. Glasses hid the eyes but the face gave the impression of isolation and bewilderment.

The nurse said, 'Your visitor' and Mrs Noakes turned uncertainly. Her sight had obviously deteriorated.

Anna said, 'Mrs Noakes,' and the old woman's mouth worked and a tear appeared on her cheek. Cheer up,' the nurse said kindly, and to Anna, 'We haven't much space for visitors but there's a small room near the door where you can talk.'

Eyes were watching from a big sitting-room on one side of the hall. The nurse led to a small room with a polished floor, a few chairs and nothing much else. The nurse guided Mrs Noakes to a chair, gave Anna a meaning smile as to a fellow guardian, and went out shutting the door. Anna drew her chair up to Mrs Noakes who was still sniffing . . .

'You're all right, aren't you?'

Mrs Noakes said, 'Damn buggers.'

'Isn't this a comfortable place?'

'Bloody hell,' Mrs Noakes said.

In the next half hour Anna was made to feel the shock of entering a 'home'. It was a place, according to Mrs Noakes, worse than prison. You had to get up, go to bed and eat when you were told, and 'they' didn't like you to smoke. The meals were uneatable – nasty uncooked salad stuff and often plain apples instead of pudding. 'When I think of them grilled steaks and boiled puddings of the old days – how they filled you up . . .' Tears came again. And there was nothing to do and nowhere to go. But worst of all were the lah-di-dah bitches. Mrs Noakes had to share a bedroom with three devils. They thought they were duchesses and looked down on her as a publican's wife. One bitch was always saying that pubs encouraged drunkenness. Mrs Noakes's bad eye-sight made things worse, as she couldn't always tell whether they were being nasty or not. But they meant it most of the time. 'I'd knock their blooming blocks off if I could see better.'

And it was Anna who had persuaded her to come to this place. 'You said as how it was like a hotel, but you hadn't seen it.'

Anna could only say, 'I'd heard it wasn't bad. Dr Gregg . . .'

'He comes and talks pretty, but he don't see half of it.' She added, 'I'd cut me throat if I could.'

Anna could only say, 'I'm sorry. I'll see what I can do.' They talked for half an hour, and then the nurse came to conduct Mrs Noakes to tea, and the old woman began to sniff again. Anna took her hand and said, 'I'll be back as soon as I can,' and then asked the nurse if she could see the matron.

In the hall the old ladies were shuffling from their large sitting-room with its chairs round the walls. Anna waited wondering what she herself would do if she lived there. 'I could read at least,' she thought and then remembered that Mrs Noakes could not read because of bad sight.

The matron saw Anna in ten minutes. She was middle-aged and friendly in a small office with family photographs on her desk – quite different from the starchy matrons of legend. But she did not provide much comfort for Mrs Noakes.

Anna must realise, the matron said, that it was a shock for every old person to leave a familiar home and possessions to come here. Nowadays there were tranquillisers to help them to settle down. 'But we don't like to use them too much as they take away the personality.' The first weeks were, of course, the worst.

She admitted that the home was crowded. There was such a need for places that the committee that had reviewed the building had squeezed in as many as possible. As for things to do, the home had been in existence only a few months, but she was hoping to build up a panel of 'friends' who would visit. The home already had hymn-singing on Sunday afternoons. 'And we wish we had more people like you who would call.'

When Anna mentioned Dr Gregg the matron said that he appreciated the difficulties. 'And he's good with the old ladies. You could have a word with him.'

It was in a way a penance to go back to the doctor. He had hinted at problems, but she, Anna, had accused him of being bureaucratic; and he had not replied to her note of apology. All the same, something had to be done about Mrs Noakes. Uncomfortably Anna telephoned and asked if she could see Laurence again and was relieved when he said, quite cordially, 'Come when you like.' He did not seen to harbour grudges, though later she was to find that he was not the iron character that she had thought.

Anyhow on this occasion he received her politely as usual after the evening surgery, and made no reference to past arguments. She described Mrs Noakes's misery, and he said, 'She was a little sorry for herself when I saw her. Some of the insults she complains of were obviously imaginary.'

That was the old judicial tone which irritated Anna, but this time she did not criticise. She said, 'Imaginary or not, she's really unhappy. Can't something be done?'

He enquired, 'What do you suggest?'

'Move her.'

He said patiently, 'Where to?'

'Isn't that for you to decide?'

He sat thinking and said at last, 'Mrs Noakes is no longer able to live on her own. That means some kind of home or hospital. I don't know of a place for her elsewhere, and if I did and she was moved she would have the same problem of settling down.'

Anna admired him a little then. He was not at that moment the lonely figure in a big gloomy house but the professional man, impersonal, with a balanced judgment. She appealed. 'I've promised to help. What can I do?'

He considered again. 'I think the best thing is to wait a little. Go and see her as often as you can, and I'll have a word with her too.'

She did not stay long, but she left with the pleasant feeling of being soothed. Laurence might be solitary and dull as a man, but he was a good doctor.

She had not yet registered with a London doctor. The next evening she wrote and asked if she might register as his patient.

The May week-end which Anna spent at home was to have unexpected consequences, but it began much as usual – Dad kissing her and saying that she was growing too elegant for him, her mother having a long conversation over the supper washing-up. They were used to unburdening their hearts in the kitchen, and Mrs Dean was frank as usual about her puzzle and doubts over Hughie, who was training at Warburton's, the firm making plastic goods. But Anna had always kept a small part of herself from her mother, and now said not a word about Tristram. She had a feeling that he would not like the friendship to be made public.

A new subject was Edward Carey. Mrs Dean said 'I'll take you out to see him tomorrow.' In a short time a close friendship had developed with the Ladyhill people. Dad did not mind of course. He admired most of the things that his wife did, and she cemented their union by taking it for granted that it was as important to mend a fuse as to read Henry James. She bolstered Dad up in every way in the house and worked with him at the family factory, and their union was solid. All the same she seemed to have found some kind of soul companion in Edward, and she was now going out to see him about once a fortnight.

'It will be a change from London,' Mrs Dean said. They left Dad and Hughie watching television sport and caught two buses and came out to green hedges and lilac. It was a windy chilly day, but the Careys' gardens, though slightly dishevelled – 'Can't keep the weeds down,' Edward said – had great clumps of peony and iris. They walked round the gardens and glass-houses with Edward limping along with his stick. Anna had an impression of something she had not expected – humility. He pointed out defects rather than beauties while the women exclaimed at the flowers. Mrs Dean did most of the talking.

They went in because of the wind and then Mrs Dean, like any mother, showed Anna off, saying that she was not only doing her Fleet Street job well but continuing the family tradition of social work in her spare time. Anna was silent, embarrassed, and after a little Mrs Dean pulled herself up. She had sharper observation than many mothers, and she said, 'The poor girl's not used to having a mother around. You talk Anna.'

Edward said almost enviously, 'I suppose you have a chance to study problems that don't touch us here.'

The problem of Mrs Noakes was still on Anna's mind and she began to talk about it and old people's homes. She described the Garden Home with its four to a bedroom and the big sitting-room with chairs round the walls, where residents sat but had nothing to do. She reported Mrs Noakes's tears and the doctor's opinion that there was no simple solution. At the end Mrs Dean wanted to hear about the doctor. Did Anna know him well? He had met the Ladyhill boys and been kind to them at the Boat Race and had mentioned Anna to Benedict. But Edward broke in. 'Do you think that small gifts would do any good?'

It seemed incongruous in a way before that vast problem of old age. But Anna was haunted by the nightmare of empty days with nothing to look forward to. She answered, 'I suppose they might break the monotony,' and Edward said, 'Give me the address.' Mrs Dean told Anna later that he was no politician and like a countryman was inclined to want things to stay as they were, but he was troubled by other people's misfortunes and in a Victorian way sent small sums of money when he heard of need. He did not speak of these, but Rose Webb, the friend who have moved to Yorkshire, had told Mrs Dean.

The three talked without a break, and at the end Anna was

introduced to the rest of the family and invited to come again. She said to her mother afterwards, 'There's a kind of out-of-the-world atmosphere about the place. They're lucky.' But Mrs Dean said, 'Edward thinks too lucky.'

But then on the next day the modern world came back to Anna with a shock.

She had hardly seen Hughie, her 'little brother' that week-end, and he had kept away for most of her visits home. Yet in their childhood she had been his second mother, as Mrs Dean said. Mrs Dean herself had been doing welfare work at the factory since her girlhood, and she had continued after marriage. Anna's memory of her was of an amusing opinionated person who was always in a hurry and was away from home for hours. Mrs Dean allowed herself no relaxation except half an hour for reading after Dad had gone to bed.

So it had fallen to Anna, the 'lieutenant colonel', to look after Hughie. He was almost five years younger, and she trained him and taught him to read, though he preferred his fleet of toy cars to books. Dad had said that Hughie was like him, while Anna was like her mother, and certainly, while Anna was good at lessons, Hughie was not much interested. He would have liked to leave school at sixteen, but Mrs Dean had arranged for him to have an extra year so that he could gain a few GCE passes. He had managed four, and Mrs Dean had said that if he had worked a little more he might have been almost as good as Anna. But, though he had many friends, he seemed relieved to be free.

There was no question about his future. He would join Dad at the firm. But Mrs Dean had thought he should have a period away from the family works, and Dad knew one of the directors of Warburton's, the large place that made plastic goods. The director had said that the boy might get some training in the management department, and Hughie had been sent there in the autumn. He had always been docile and made no objection, but since then, Mrs Dean told Anna, 'we've hardly been able to get a word out of him.' He did not tell them what he was doing, and he was out with friends in most of his spare time.

'Parents shouldn't pry too much,' Mrs Dean said, but she discussed Hughie every time that Anna came home. Anna herself, among all the new experiences of London, wondered a little about Hughie. Had she gone away when he needed her?

That Sunday morning the boy had not appeared for breakfast, and Mrs Dean said, 'We never see him till midday Sunday.' In spite of her strong views about not prying, she wondered if Anna could get something out of him. 'Clean socks,' she said at eleven on the Sunday. 'Take them up and see what he's doing.'

Anna knocked and said, 'Clean socks.' The room was dark, and she went across and pulled the curtains. One eye peeped out from the sheets. She said, 'Lazybones. Why don't you get up?'

'It's Sunday,' he muttered.

She came and sat heavily on the side of the bed. The sheet was pushed back a little more, and a tousled head appeared. 'Is breakfast over?'

'Of course it is. What are you doing at Warburton's?'

There was a pause, and then he said, 'Nothing.'

'Little idiot. You can't have been doing nothing for eight months.'

'They give me papers to look at and typing for their beastly house journal, and that's all.'

'Why don't you ask for work?'

'They're all old men,' he muttered.

'Then why don't you tell Mother and Dad?'

'They were so keen on Warburton's.'

Anna was suddenly angry. 'Look here. You can't expect other people to push you all the time. You must make some effort yourself.'

He had always taken her orders without resentment. Now he sat up in bed, round-faced, fair and docile. 'All right. You needn't shout. I'll talk to Mother.'

Anna felt a little spurt of pride that she could still influence him and said, 'You know that everybody's fond of you.' She went to his drawer and put away the socks and paused at the muddle. Socks, handkerchiefs, ties, letters and cough lozenges were tangled together. 'What an awful drawer,' she said, and then saw, hidden in a corner, a crumpled piece of paper with some white pills. 'Hughie,' she said, her voice rising, 'what have you got here?'

'Nothing,' he said hastily.

'What are they?'

'Don't know. Some girls gave them to me.'

'My God,' Anna said. 'You haven't been taking them.'

'Only two.'

She knew nothing of the drug cult except what she read in the papers. She was horrified. At the back of her mind was the thought that, if she had been at home, he might have been protected. And now she was going off again the next morning.

She picked up the crumpled paper with the tips of her fingers. 'I'll get rid of these. Hughie swear to me that you won't take any more.'

'All right,' he said ashamed. 'They don't seem to do much anyhow.'

But that was not enough. She must ensure that he kept his word. She said, 'I'll tell you what. Come and have a week-end with me in London, and we can talk things over.'

'OK,' he said in his docile way.

But that still was not enough. 'When will you come?'

'Oh some time.'

'No. I want a date. Come in a fortnight – my long week-end. Mind you do.'

'All right,' he said again, but she did not quite trust him. 'I'll tell Mother we've fixed it. She'll see that you come.'

He said, 'All right,' yet again and slid out of bed. 'But I won't tell her about these,' Anna said, taking the pills. 'It would worry her to death.' She paused at the door. 'Hughie, *don't* make a fool of yourself,' and felt the old tenderness for the boy who looked so young. She took the pills to the dustbin and hid them deep among the rubbish. Mrs Dean was in the kitchen. 'You've been a long time up there. Is he all right?'

'Not really. But he's promised to talk to you. And he says he'll have a week-end with me in London – in a fortnight. See he does, won't you?'

'You're a good little lieutenant colonel,' Mrs Dean said. 'You're always successful.'

Anna was to think of the irony of this later.

It was Thursday, Anna's day for meeting Tristram. All day she had been thinking how she would tell him about Hughie. He might make one of those unconventional comments which, when considered afterwards, threw a fresh light on baffling situations. He seemed never to accept a conventional view. Perhaps it was his life abroad that made him stand aside and refuse accepted opinions. At first, Anna thought, one violently disagreed with him, but then, after thinking his judgments over, one might – at least she might – come to the conclusion that he was right. It was this that partly made their meetings so precious, but of course there was much more – this feeling of love which made meeting him like coming home.

He was pale on that summer evening, but she had seen him pale at other times. When she asked after his health he always depreciated himself. 'I'm not exactly a Hercules, you know.' Most people are interested in themselves and like to talk about their situations and personalities. Tristram, it seemed, did not think himself worth discussion. And yet he must have known that he had a marvellous gift of words.

They met in the usual way and collected their rolls and coffee and sat facing one another, and she breathed a sigh of relief that they were together again. She asked. 'Did you have a nice week-end?'

He did not answer, and she thought he might think her over-curious. So she began to tell him about Hughie, and he disposed himself to listen with his usual interest. She told him of finding the pills in the drawer. 'I was horrified.'

She expected him to be horrified too, but he made one of his perverse comments. 'One has to experiment sometimes.'

'What? With those things?'

He said meditatively, 'We're blind on our own.'

She cried, still horrified, 'You don't take such things, do you?'

'I might if I knew of anything one could trust. But one doesn't know.'

She said indignantly, 'You're not suggesting that I should encourage Hughie to take drugs? He's only just eighteen and young for his age.'

'I'm not suggesting anything. Only wondering.' Then as usual he turned the conversation away from himself. 'Why is Hughie young for his age?'

'He's always been. We've always had to push him.'

'May not the pushing be just the reason?'

'How could it be? We *try* to make him grow up.'

'And enjoy directing him?'

'Maybe.' She suddenly saw that she enjoyed exercising authority. Tristram always punctured self-conceit. She thought, 'He talks about being blind, yet he's sensitive to things we ourselves just don't see.' She dared herself to say, 'He's coming up for the week-end. Could you – would you – meet him and see for yourself?'

But it seemed that even that humble request was too much. She got one of those replies that would darken her evening. 'Why don't you ask that doctor friend of yours?'

She flushed and said hotly, 'He isn't really a friend at all.'

'I'm sorry,' he said. He was quick to apologise when she seemed hurt. There was a silence. Then he made an obvious effort. 'My father died on Monday.'

'*What?*'

'I'm a bit involved in his affairs.'

She was aghast. All that argument over Hughie while he had been coping with death. It hurt her too that he had not told her at once.

'*Tristram.* Why didn't you tell me?'

'I thought you wanted to talk.'

'Of course I don't if you're in trouble. Oh I'm so sorry, I didn't know he was ill.'

'He wasn't. He seemed quite happy last Saturday with his books and societies.' Still speaking in a quiet neutral way he told her that the charwoman had found his father in the garden when she went in on the Monday morning. 'He'd had some heart trouble.'

'And you?'

'I'd been in Sussex for the week-end.'

She cried out in sympathy, 'Such a shock!'

He said quite calmly, 'My two aunts who live near are helping.'

'And I can't do anything in any way?'

'Who can?'

Anna had never had anybody very close to her die, but she thought, if she had, she would talk about it interminably and beg for sympathy. Was Tristram unusual in behaving so quietly? Yet he had always spoken of his father affectionately.

Was it some dissatisfaction with this world or some glimpse of something beyond it that made him accept death like this – without surprise? In any case was it not morbid to dwell on these things instead of getting on with the business of living? Round her were the chattering summer crowds, all with their interests and friends. Was that not better than sitting, as he was doing, looking at death and taking it as part of existence?

Then she looked at his pensive handsome face and thought, 'Of course he is immeasurably superior. If I could only bring him a bit closer.' This was her problem – somehow to make him feel more for the things of this world; for her. A show of sympathy was no good. 'Perhaps,' she thought, 'If I'm patient . . .'

She dared a little. 'You needn't have come.'

'What good would that have done?'

It sounded like indifference but it might have been kindness. For when she asked trembling, 'You'll go on living at Hampstead, won't you?' he said, 'I'll be there for the present anyhow.'

And at the end, when she turned the screw on herself and said, 'You won't want to come next week,' he said, 'The funeral will be over. I shall be free,' and she was filled with warm gratitude. That was what was always happening at their meetings – unhappiness at his remoteness and then thankfulness for his kindness. But whatever the meetings brought, she was helpless. At that first sight she had known that he would influence the rest of her life. She said as they parted, 'I do appreciate you, you know,' which was a strange ending to an announcement of death.

Old Jack looked in on the morning that Anna was expecting Hughie. The old man had become a friend, whether with the doctor's knowledge or not she did not know, and did small jobs for her such as putting in a high light-bulb or making a window-box. He was of great use. The only disadvantage was that he talked interminably.

Now she said, 'I can't spare the time today. I'm expecting my brother and I've got a sore throat.'

Jack said, 'Why don't you go to the doctor?'

'Doctor? No. I'm far too busy.'

He went and she began to prepare the dinner. She suspected that the sore throat might have been caused by exasperation. Hughie had not come on the day fixed. Mrs Dean had rung up to say that they were having discussions on Warburton's and Hughie seemed a bit upset. 'He shall come the next week-end when things are more settled.'

Anna had agreed but then remembered that that week-end was her short break, when she worked on Sunday evening. Oh well, she would have to pack the boy off when she went to work.

Mrs Dean had not known what time he would arrive. It was always difficult to get him up at the week-end. But there would be no need to meet him at Euston. The journey to Waterloo Station was easy and Anna had given him a street map.

So now, grumbling at the boy's vagueness, she prepared a large meal and waited. The hours went by. She was at first glad to have a rest; then angry and finally anxious. At nearly five she was about to telephone Birmingham when there was a ring at her door. She went down relieved but angry and then drew back. There were two figures at the door.

With Hughie was a girl in red. She was tall, buxom, with a wide mouth and long black hair. From her came a waft of perfume and cigarettes.

She seemed to tower over Hughie who said timidly, 'This is Carol. We've come up together.'

Anna could only say 'Come in.' She opened the door of her small room for them to leave their cases and, kept from anger by the stranger, said 'I've put away dinner. I suppose you want tea.'

Hughie muttered something about the journey's taking longer than they had thought. Anna left them and went to get the tea. When she returned to the sitting-room with a tray they were sitting side by side at her table by the window, and the girl had her hand, with its long painted nails, on Hughie's. Anna thought that she was probably in her mid-twenties, but it was difficult to tell as she had plastered her face with make-up. She dwarfed the boy and kept her attitude of possession as Anna went and came. Finally, as Anna brought in the tea-pot the girl sat up a little, and Anna said, 'Well?'

Again it was Hughie who answered timidly. 'We're going to work in London.'

'*What?*'

The girl broke in with a Birmingham voice. 'We're a-going to get engaged and work together. I'll find a job as a waitress and Hugh says he'll do the washing-up. Hugh thought you'd let us stay here till we got a room.'

The two were eating as if they were starved. Hughie mumbled, 'We didn't get any lunch at Euston. It cost an awful lot.'

Anna began to laugh, and the girl's red shoe with its high heel pressed against Hughie's sandal. She said fiercely, 'It ain't a joke. We mean it. We ain't going back to Warburton's no more.'

Anna turned to Hughie, 'Have you told Mother?'

'Not yet,' he mumbled.

'You left home without a word?'

'She knew that I wanted to leave Warburton's and that I was coming to you.'

Their escapade, which had seemed comic, began to look serious. Anna asked the girl, 'Does your family know about this?'

'I don't live with no family.'

'But you work at Warburton's.'

'Like him I did.'

'Did you tell them that you were leaving?'

The girl took out a packet of cigarettes, offered it to Anna who shook her head, said, 'You don't mind me having one,' and lighted up.

'But Warburton's,' Anna insisted.

'We don't bother about them. People are always leaving.'

'Where are you going to look for a room?'

The girl spoke more politely. 'Hugh says you know London and would help.'

Hughie shifted uneasily. 'I didn't exactly say . . .'

'Well really,' Anna exclaimed but with a growing sense of helplessness. Hughie had another boss now, and she, Anna, was no match for this girl. It was two against one, and there was no wiser person to talk sense. Then the doorbell rang down below, and she was glad to escape for a moment.

It was Dr Gregg. He said hesitantly, 'Jack says you aren't well.'

She was flooded with relief. Here might be an ally. She had forgotten her sore throat and said, 'I'm all right but I've got a crisis on.'

He said, 'Shall I go away?' but she drew him outside where the two upstairs could not hear and whispered details. 'If you could just come up and talk to them.'

The room was full of smoke and Carol was leaning on Hughie's shoulder. Seeing the tall man at the door, however, she sat up. Anna introduced them. 'This is Carol and this is my brother Hughie. They want to leave their Birmingham jobs and work in a London café.' Then she went out to get another cup to give the doctor tea.

When she returned Laurence seemed to be looking them over meditatively. He was asking, 'How long have you two been together?'

Carol said defiantly, 'Some time,' but Hughie corrected her innocently, 'No. It's only a few weeks, but Carol wants to look after me.'

'So,' the doctor said to Carol, 'he isn't responsible.'

She tossed back her hair and said, 'I don't know what you mean.'

'You do.' He was now in charge and Anna had only to watch. 'Who was your previous boyfriend?'

Suddenly Anna saw a gleam of light. Carol was tall and she wore a loose red dress, and she, Anna, had not noticed her figure. But Laurence Gregg was a doctor. He said to Anna, 'Can we have another window open? All this smoke doesn't do a pregnancy any good.'

'Pregnancy,' Hughie said wonderingly. 'What pregnancy?'

Nobody answered, but Laurence said to Carol, 'I'm a doctor. You can tell me what you like.' He was authoritative and yet, Anna thought, he was not unsympathetic. Slowly he broke down Carol's resistance. She said at first, 'You can't force me to say anything, you know,' but then put down her cigarette and in jerks, in answer to the doctor's questions, gave details of a depressing life story. Anna, listening, realised that the girl was intelligent and that Hughie had not been such a complete fool to be attracted. Hughie himself sat hunched, silent with shock.

Carol had had no father and did not remember her mother. She had been put into care before she was two, and had spent all her childhood in one barmy place after another with soppy old women looking for nits in your hair and creating a fuss because the girls made eyes at the milkman. She had apparently been too wild to be considered for fostering, and she had run away several times. She had got a bad name, and the old dames at her last home had told the teachers at her school, and so she had got a bad name there too. Everybody seemed to hate her, but she had escaped at sixteen and did all sorts of jobs, but she hadn't gone near the red light district in Birmingham.

Of course she knew a lot of chaps. She wasn't sure who was the father of the coming baby. She had thought of having an abortion, but it had seemed a bit of a shame, especially as some of her boy friends were clever. And then she had waited too long and now the child must be four or five months on the way.

She had not meant any harm to Hugh. He had told her that he liked babies and she thought he might like to be a father. She would have worked to the last minute anyway. She did not know that he was as young as eighteen.

As she ran through her story she seemed to realise that her venture was a failure. She tossed back her hair again and sat upright with tight lips. Anna thought that she might be near tears, but she was not going to betray any emotion. The doctor who had won a victory showed no triumph. He was frowning and seemed to be trying to think of a way out. He said at last, 'What do you want to do?'

She got up. 'Well, that's that.'

'Where are you going?'

'Don't know. But I'm not staying where I'm not wanted.'

At last the doctor spoke sharply. 'Stop being foolish. We've got to find somewhere for you to go. It's too late to return to Birmingham tonight.'

Carol, dropping the last of her defiance, said, 'No good going back. I told the woman I wouldn't be wanting the rooms no longer.'

'There must be a few other places in Birmingham,' the doctor said with some irony. Then Anna, warm with relief, came into the conversation. 'I've got only one spare room, but one of us could sleep on the floor.'

But the doctor turned to Carol. 'You'd better have a comfortable night. I'll get my nurse to come over and make you up a bed in my house. I'd like to talk to you a bit more.'

He was a saviour, a law-giver. Never would Anna call him dull again. She murmured thanks and he said, 'You look after your brother.' Carol gave Hughie a pat on the shoulder, said, 'So long,' and went to get her case. Anna had a suspicion that she might not be unwilling to have a night in a doctor's house. She followed Laurence down the stairs, and Anna opened the door. The doctor said, 'We'll talk again in the morning,' took Carol's case and walked off with her into the dusk. Silence descended.

It was Hughie who probably suffered most. He was still sitting by the window and said nothing. Anna, remembering Tristram's words about not giving him orders, also said nothing, but carried the tea-things out and washed up. When she returned he was asleep looking, with his corn-coloured hair and round face, the picture of innocence.

The doctor telephoned at nine the next morning saying that Carol had agreed to return to Birmingham. What was Anna's brother going to do?

'I'll ask him,' Anna said. Hughie was still in bed – hiding from a hard world, Anna thought – but she had issued no commands as she might have done in the past. Now she only said. 'The doctor's on the phone. Carol wants to go back.'

He sat up but did not meet her eye. 'I suppose I'd better go too.'

She returned to the telephone. 'He says he'll go too. Can they be trusted together, do you think? I've got to work this afternoon.'

She had angled for it of course, but she expressed polite concern when he said he could go with them. Might he not be wanted? But he said that Jack would stay in, and he, Laurence, had a substitute in an emergency. There was a train from Euston at eleven. He would call with Carol just after ten.

After that it was all haste – getting Hughie up and giving him breakfast. They hardly spoke; only Anna said, 'Talk to Mother. I'll phone her when you've gone.'

Carol looked older when she arrived with the doctor. She had removed most of her make-up and was heavy-eyed. It was a brief meeting. The doctor said, 'Ready?' Hughie silently clumped down the stairs. Anna said, 'Cheer up, old boy,' and he gave her a wan smile. Carol only said to Anna, 'So long,' and they departed, the doctor between the two like a father with two children.

Anna, weary and thankful for solitude, rang up her mother. Mrs Dean, generally short and brisk on the telephone, talked more than usual, a sign that she was worried. She knew nothing of Carol, and reported only that Hughie had left at nine in the morning and had said nothing about his movements. He had been silent altogether recently with this trouble over Warburton's.

Anna, remembering Tristram again, said, 'Haven't we been bossing him about too much?'

'You've been the chief boss,' Mrs Dean said. But she agreed that she would be a 'sucking dove' in future. 'Dad is one already.' She would also provide lunch for the three and see what she could do for Carol.

'Righto,' Anna said. She did not pay her mother compliments, but she thought, 'What must it be like to have no mother?' – a feeling that was later to grow and influence her life. She said to herself that morning, 'No wonder there are Carols.'

That evening the doctor telephoned half an hour after she had got back from work. He gave a short account of what had happened. Carol and Hughie had hardly spoken to one another. Carol had gone into the corridor and turned her back on them. Hughie, in contrast, had talked quite a lot – about cricket and cars and his old school. 'A juvenile still,' the doctor said. 'Perhaps this affair will grow him up. But a nice boy. One can understand why Carol fixed on him.'

Carol herself seemed to know absolutely nothing about the process of birth or child care. Mrs Dean had promised to talk to her. 'You have an intelligent mother,' Laurence said.

Mrs Dean had given them lunch and had mentioned a local home for unmarried mothers that might suit Carol. 'I left them together,' the doctor said. He has stayed with the Deans only two hours and must have had a strenuous day. Yet he seemed curiously pleased. This was not, it turned out, only because he had been kind and successful, and not only because he had been of service to Anna, though that was part of it. It was because he had been back to the Midlands, which he had not seen for years. 'I thought I detested Birmingham, but I found I had an odd affection for the place though it's been knocked about a lot. Those solid red-brick Edgbaston houses – many of them are ugly of course but they reminded me of the old prosperous days before unemployment.'

He talked more than he had ever talked before. Anna listened and made polite comments, but she was tired and she wished that he would stop. He seemed to realise this after a time and said, 'I apologise for talking too long. Go early to bed and don't worry.'

'If,' she thought, 'Tristram said that kind of thing to me . . .' Her thoughts always went the same way. But that did not stop her from being grateful to Laurence. There was some comfort in having a protective presence five minutes away.

Jos and his daughter Irene were at the pottery. He went there to work for a few hours each day, and sometimes Irene accompanied him, especially in the last few weeks when Jenny had not come to play with her. While he threw pots at the back she sat at the front-room table rapidly covering sheets of paper with coloured drawings. Sometimes he let her make small clay men with round heads and bodies and small circles in front for buttons. He baked them for her, but the heads generally fell off.

Her love of drawing amazed him. There had been some talent in his Kentish grandmother's family, but it had missed his father and brother and come out in him only in decorating his pottery. It amazed him anyhow that this small girl with wispy fair hair and a look of Helena should be his daughter.

In his bachelor days when he compared himself with other men he had lamented that he had no sons. The two boys, Benedict Carey and Alan Owen, had in a way acted as sons for a short period, and Benedict, away at Cambridge, still sometimes came to talk in his vacations. But the idea of having a daughter had never been there. And now this child, not yet five years old, seemed to have inherited family talent that he hardly knew was there. She had also inherited his childhood timidity. Helena said that Irene was more his child than hers.

He came out from the back now to find half-a-dozen sheets scattered over the table. They were covered with outlines in bright colours with wavering capital letters beside them. Helena had already taught Irene her letters. The child drew heads of pigs and horses in imitation of Jenny's own drawings, crenellated castles with flags, flying from Helena's stories, flowers in pots from the family glasshouses and thin trailing shapes with large eyes which she labelled 'Gost'. There was also a figure with large feet and orange hair.

'Who's that?'

'Hughie what mends cars.' Since he had left Warburton's Hughie had passed his driving test and had brought his mother to Ladyhill in the family car. While Mrs Dean talked to Edward, Hughie had retired to look at the old Carey car and with Jos's permission had made adjustments.

Jos said now, 'Do you like him?'

'He's sad.'

'But you aren't sad, are you?' Remembering his own unhappy childhood Jos had asked her this question several times.

'Only because Jenny doesn't come any more.'

Jos thought, 'I must speak to Helena. We're punishing Irene by keeping Jenny out.' He said, 'She's staying away because of all that trouble when Crabby had to bring you home. But we'll tell Jenny to come back, shall we?'

Dismissing a delicate subject, he looked at her drawings again. 'Why do you keep on drawing ghosts? They aren't real.'

'Jenny says they are.'

'Jenny says a lot of funny things.'

But she capped his remonstrance with the simple statement, 'I've seed them.' And he remembered the terrors of his own childhood and how he never told anybody about them. Was it the same with her? Trying to shield her he said, 'Listen dearie. You be brave and the nasty things will go away.'

'Girls can't be brave.'

'Of course they can. What about Red Riding Hood?'

'But the wolf came.'

'The wolf was killed in the end.'

She considered this. 'But you can't kill ghosts.'

'You can tell them to go away.'

She sighed. 'Don't like talking to them. They've got big eyes.'

'Have a go and see what happens.' He thought they had talked enough about childhood fears and added, 'I know you're a brave girl really. I wonder what there is for dinner.'

Irene gathered up her drawings. They would go home for Helena to see. She said, 'I think I'm a bit hungry.'

'Come on then.' He moved to the back to clear up. 'And you show us how brave you can be.' They went out and he locked the door. Then he crouched so that she could climb on to his back, and she put her small hands over his shoulders and her small legs round his waist, and he rose and pranced through the village while she shouted 'Charge. Charge.'

All that day Irene pondered on her father's command that she must be brave.

That evening, sleeping in Benedict's room, she tried in the summer twilight to stare hard at the monsters round her and found, if she looked long enough, they stopped being monsters and became ordinary pieces of furniture. She listened to the movements and voices downstairs, and thought how there were only about twenty stairs between her and them, and she heard cars going by outside and thought, 'I'm safe' and went to sleep quite quickly.

She felt very brave the next morning. Millie took her down to the shop, but Jenny was at school. Millie talked to Jenny's father who seemed pleased because Alan was coming home from London for the week-end and bringing a doctor friend. He asked Millie to tell them at The Hollies. He gave Irene some jelly sweets and said that she was getting a big girl. That made her feel braver than ever.

In the afternoon she was alone in the garden and thinking how she could be brave. The most obvious place was the Iron House behind the elder bushes where Jenny said ghosts from the churchyard gathered. Generally Irene shut her eyes and ran by it, but now, she thought, she would go and look at it, and if the ghosts were there she would tell them to go away.

No Jenny was there to go with her, but she was brave and went alone. She did not tell anybody in case she might be stopped, and unseen she ran down to the main road. She passed the shop where all the customers had their backs turned to the road, past the way to the pottery, the public house and the school and came finally to a field and the elder trees in front of the Iron House. They were in thick leaf and the white circles of flowers above Irene's head with their strong sweet smell were just fading and they gave an air of dusty mystery to the side of the road.

Irene pushed through and looked squarely at the Iron House. It was made of corrugated iron, and there was rust at the corners and along the top of the shut door in the middle of the front side. It had been empty for years, and there were webs and old brown leaves at the edge of the corrugated roof.

Nothing seemed to stir behind the elder trees. Irene stood a moment and then charged with all her strength at the door. It did not fit well and there were cracks round it and it creaked and the top bent inward. She tried again with her hands in front of her like a battering ran and then pushed with her shoulder and a small gap appeared round the edge. At last it creaked open a little, enough for her to put a foot through the gap. Then she pushed again and got through.

She looked round. There seemed to be no ghosts there that afternoon. There was only a floor of dusty cracked concrete with bird droppings here and there. She leaned against the door and looked up. There were bits of nests in corners, and lines of light sloped down from holes in the corrugated iron roof. The place was dark after the sun outside and it had a mouldy smell, but there was nothing there to frighten people.

There was nothing to wait for and she must get back for tea. She turned to go out, but in leaning against the half-open door she had pushed it to. It was made to open inward, and now there was only a crack of light along its sides.

Irene dug her small nails into the crack to pull the door open, but she could not move it. She persisted for a long time, but she hurt her nails and could not widen the crack. So she stopped and stood to consider. She was not afraid. She could hear the faint whirr of traffic along the road, and she knew that her parents would come to look for her. So she began to bang on the iron wall of the front. If she had had a stick she could have made a big rattling noise but her fists made only a small boom. Then her fists grew sore; so she sat down in a corner to wait.

The light through the holes in the roof began to turn golden. Slowly the dusk came on, and now Irene was cold and hungry, and she wanted to go to the lavatory. With a sense of shame she went to another corner and pulled down her knickers. Then she began again to bang on the front and shout, 'I'm here. I'm here,' but nobody came. Shouting made her thirsty; so she stopped and went back to her first corner, and huddled up against the side. Then it got quite dark, and she fell asleep.

She slipped sideways, half woke, cold and stiff, several times and sank back to sleep. It was light when she finally woke, but it must have been early because the road seemed silent. For some time there was only a bird twittering. But then the whirr of cars began again, and with legs that did not work very well she limped to the front and began banging again. But still nobody came; so she went back to her corner and dozed. Voices outside waked her and she sat up and shouted. But she had been too slow and they had gone away.

After that she spent the day between banging and dozing. Sometimes she wanted to cry, but her father had said she must be brave and she had no handkerchief. Later she did not think about being brave or think of anything much. The day grew warmer but she did not know the time or how many hours had gone by. She just lay in her corner watching the light grow golden again and then dusk coming.

But then something lovely happened. The ghosts arrived, but they did not have staring eyes, but were beautiful ladies with long floating hair and soft drifting robes. They were kind like mothers, and they bent over her, and she said, 'Who are you?' And one said, 'We're not from the churchyard but from a wonderful land far away, and we've come to put you to sleep.' The lady spread out a silky soft cover and wrapped Irene in it. And Irene said, 'I'll never be afraid of you again,' and she went straight to sleep once more.

The Owens had been looking forward with some trepidation to Dr Gregg's visit. Alan had suggested inviting him to Ladyhill that weekend as they had become friendly and there was even talk of Alan joining the doctor's practice when the boy qualified. Alan had said that the doctor came from Solihull but had been unhappy and had kept away from the Midlands for years. Now Alan wanted to give him a good impression.

Mrs Owen said, 'We'll give him a good dinner anyway,' and worked hard in the kitchen. Jenny did the dusting when she returned from school. She was to let the doctor have her room and was going, as in the old days, to sleep in Gran's cottage. She hoped her mother would tell the doctor that she was moving out for him so that he would think her a self-sacrificing girl. Alan had talked a lot about the doctor and she wanted to charm him.

And then all the happy preparations became sawdust. Somebody said in the shop that there seemed to be some trouble at The Hollies, and then there was a loud banging on the side door and there was Helena, dishevelled and glaring. She did not even say good afternoon but cried. 'Where is Jenny?' Unfortunately Jenny was there helping to make a trifle. Helena saw her before she could escape and shouted, 'What have you done with Irene?'

Jenny stood open-mouthed, too much frightened to answer. Even the pacific Mrs Owen said, 'It's no use frightening the child.' Helena made an effort to control herself and said to Mrs Owen, 'Sorry. But she must know something.'

'Is Irene lost then?' Mrs Owen said, and Helena said in a hoarse voice, 'We've searched for hours.'

Mrs Owen's eyes went moist. She was fond of Irene. 'Oh you poor thing,' she said. 'I wish we could help.' And she said to Jenny, but quite gently, 'Do you know anything Jen?' But Jenny shook her head speechless.

'She came straight home from school,' Mrs Owen said. 'You know she doesn't go up to see Irene now.'

But Helena cried, 'She played tricks before. One can't believe a word she says.'

There was silence after that dreadful speech. Then Jenny, to her own embarrassment, began to cry. It was not only Irene's disappearance but the bitterness of being barred from The Hollies and behind that Benedict's scorn. Everything in her home life had gone wrong. Her mother gave her a handkerchief but still her tears dripped.

Helena stood irresolute for a moment, and then said more softly, 'I'm sorry but I had to enquire,' and Jenny knew that Helena did not believe her. Mrs Owen went with her into the yard, and Jenny heard her say, 'I'll talk to her later and let you know.' And that was a humiliation – the two women talking about her as if she were a young child. Then Mrs Owen came back and half apologised for Helena, saying, 'She's terribly upset. I'm sure you don't know anything, do you?' and Jenny stopped crying, and said, 'She's a pig and I hate her.'

'Poor soul. We must help if we can,' Mrs Owen said in her kind way. But the evening was blighted, and Jenny's thoughts about charming the strange doctor faded. Her eyes would be red and Helena's bitter sentence, 'One can't believe a word she says,' remained with her. Silent she helped to finish the cooking, and then Mrs Owen said, 'Why not have some supper now and go early to bed? I expect Irene will have been found by tomorrow morning.'

So Jenny went to bed and forgot her troubles. But when she got up and looked out of the window the next morning she saw a group of village people outside the shop and knew that Irene was still lost.

Late in the morning the doctor's car drew up in front of the shop. The knot of people who had come for news looked at it suspiciously, but Alan jumped out and called to a youth that he knew, 'What on earth?' And the youth said, 'Baby from The Hollies disappeared.'

The Owens had been going to keep the trouble from their guest, but he got out and heard the conversation. Jenny in the yard had a good view of him – tall with a strong nose and chin rather like a Wild West hero, only his hair was cut short. He stood back listening until Mrs Owen came out and apologised for the crowd and invited him in.

Jenny was introduced as Alan's sister, 'but not really like me,' Alan said laughing. Alan seemed very happy to have the doctor there and called him 'Laurence'. Jenny had the feeling that he must be a great man in London, and she kept very quiet and watched him. He had an expensive watch on his bony wrist, and he seemed rather silent, listening to the Owens' story of Irene's disappearance. In a way the disappearance was a good thing, for it broke the ice of the first meeting. Then Mr Owen went back to the shop where Gran had been doing duty, and since it was a fine afternoon and the Owens wanted to show the countryside to the doctor the rest of them went for a drive to Malvern.

Jenny began to like the doctor very much. He had an expensive car and he drove smoothly – not like the tearaway young men who roared through the village.

They went slowly at first, all of them peering through the windows to see if there was any sign of Irene. But the roads, with their blackberry flowers and wild roses, seemed empty. Mrs Owen, who sat in front next to the doctor, talked about the village, and the doctor made complimentary remarks; but Alan, sitting with Jenny at the back, said that he would prefer to work as a doctor in London because it would give you wider experience.

At Malvern people were picnicking, and motor cycles were roaring about, but somehow the light-heartedness grated because Irene was still lost. They did not stop for tea but went straight back to see if there was any news. But people were still outside the shop, and they said that nothing had been heard of the child.

The Owens pretended to be more cheerful than they felt, and Mrs Owen and Jenny got a lavish tea. The doctor talked a little of Solihull where he had been brought up, but it was all rather a pretence because they were worried. After tea the doctor and Alan went for a walk. Alan said he wanted the doctor to see the Worcestershire lanes, but obviously it was partly to look for Irene.

Nobody could settle to anything. Mr Owen kept the shop open late in case any news came. Mrs Owen went up to see that the doctor's room, really Jenny's, was in order. Jenny had a plate of apple crumble, looked at television for half an hour and then took her night things over to Gran's. Gran had become rather deaf, and it took a long time to tell her about the doctor and Malvern. But their thoughts were really on one thing – the loss of Irene. Jenny went back to the shop to enquire before she washed for bed, but everybody was curiously quiet and nothing had been heard.

Jenny must have slept for about three hours when she was suddenly wide awake. Perhaps it was a dream. She did not know how she had got the message. But she saw absolutely where Irene was.

Years before she had crept from Gran's cottage at night to curse the American lady who then occupied Meadow Grange. Then it had been bright moonlight but now the sky was overcast with a faint streak of colour in the north west. The time before she had been very quiet but now she did not have to bother since Gran was conveniently deaf. Jenny could hear her heavy breathing.

Jenny flung on her dressing-gown, pulled on her bedroom slippers and opened the door. Lights were still on in some upper windows, including those of her home, and a few cars still bowled along the road. But she hardly noticed. She must get to the Iron House. She ran past the Ploughman's Arms and the school and came to a dim gap and then the elder trees.

Behind them the Iron House stood silent and apparently deserted. But Jenny pushed through the elders and saw in the faint light that the cracks round the door were wider than when she had surveyed it in the spring. Like Irene but with more strength she ran at the door and it opened a little. She peered in and there was a pale heap in a corner.

She thought it might be dead, but she did not wait to see. She left the door ajar and ran back through the village to the branching road and The Hollies. A Police car was outside, and the house lights were on. Jenny slammed the gate, ran up the path and banged frantically on the door. Helena, pale and distraught and still in her day clothes, stood there. Jenny gasped, 'She's in the Iron House by the churchyard.'

There was a sudden rush. Jos was there too. He and Helena said nothing but ran out. Jenny went after them but could hardly keep up. They ran all the way to the elder trees and broke through them and thrust at the door, and Jos strode across the floor to the bundle. He lifted it and said to Helena, 'I think she's only asleep.' And in a moment they were gone again, and Irene picked up one of Irene's sandals that had dropped.

But she kept her wits about her. There at her own home was Dr Gregg and he might be able to help. She ran and banged on the side door and her father came. 'She's found but she may be dead,' Jenny cried breathless. 'Can the doctor come?' And her father went up and called Dr Gregg who had not yet gone to bed, and he came in his shirt without his neat jacket, and Jenny said, 'I'll show you.'

There was no time to impress him. Jenny tried to keep up with his long strides, and they were at The Hollies in less than five minutes. The lights were blazing everywhere, and the front door was open, and the doctor gave a rap on the door and walked in. Millie, who also looked as if she had been crying, was in the kitchen heating something. Jenny said, 'He's a doctor,' and Millie ran upstairs. Then Jos appeared at the top of the stairs and Dr Gregg went up. Jenny handed the sandal to Millie, who took it up with some milk.

Jenny did not know whether to stay, but she wanted to know if Irene was dead, and she thought that in any case it might be rude to the doctor to go off. So she stayed in the kitchen, listening and stroking one of Millie's cats. After some time there were voices on the stairs, and Dr Gregg said, 'She'll do. Keep her warm and give her plenty to drink,' and that meant that Irene was not dead and a great weight rolled away. Helena came down with the doctor and said, 'How marvellous that you were here.' But she did not ask who had brought him.

Then she saw Jenny, and she glared and her voice rose. 'So you knew where she was all the time.'

'I didn't.' But Jenny was frightened again.

'Then how did you know tonight?'

'I went to sleep and guessed.'

It sounded silly, and Helena obviously did not believe it. Her face went hard and she said, 'We've had enough of your stories. You are never to come here again.' She took no more notice of Jenny, but said to the doctor, 'Thank God you were here,' and he said, 'I'll look in in the morning,' and Helena ran upstairs again.

The doctor glanced down at Jenny with the hint of a smile, and they went out of the front door. In the road he took her hand. She was half crying. 'I didn't know where she was. I didn't. I just guessed.' And he said kindly, 'Don't worry. Mrs Meredith is upset. It will be all right in the morning.'

Jenny said sniffing, 'Animals are much nicer than people.'

'You'd better be a vet,' the doctor said. Mrs Owen must have been talking to him about Jenny's habits. The remark was to settle Jenny's future.

Something else happened. All that bitter adoration of Benedict Carey ebbed, and she began to adore this tall man who held her hand.

He said now, 'Cheer up. After all you were the one who found the little girl,' and Jenny said in a burst of admiration, 'I wish you were our doctor.'

Now they had reached Gran's cottage, and Dr Gregg opened the door and said, 'Good night. Don't catch cold,' and went on to give the news that Irene had been found. Jenny would have given the news to Gran, but the steady breathing was still sounding upstairs. Gran had slept all through that hour that had changed Jenny's life.

The next day was unnaturally lovely. Unlike most days it was almost unmixed pleasure, once the first bit was over. It began when Jenny woke to hear her mother talking loudly as one had to do to Gran in the kitchen. 'Isn't Jen up yet?' her mother was saying.

It had been some time before Jenny had got to sleep. She had been chilly and there were so many things to think about. But as she remembered the doctor's big hand round hers she had drifted away, and now she woke like a new being. She slipped out of bed and ran down the stairs in her nightdress, and her mother said, 'Hurry up and dress. Helena has come to see you.'

That was the worst moment of the day. In ten minutes, glum and frightened, Jenny walked into the home kitchen, and there was Helena, looking thin and grey, talking to Jenny's father. She broke off and turned in quite a smiling way to Jenny and said, 'I've come to apologise.'

Jenny bit her lip, not knowing what to say.

'Irene's been telling us,' Helena said, 'that she went down to that shack all on her own. Jenny had ordered her not to go there.'

'Whatever made her?' Mr Owen asked.

'It was Jos. He had been telling her to be brave.'

'Well, and it was brave,' Mr Owen said. He always made a pleasant remark if he could.

Helena said that she must get back. 'Your blessed Dr Gregg says she's all right, but I don't like to leave her for long.' She turned back to Jenny. 'We're eternally grateful though goodness knows how you found her. I was horrible last night. Please forget it. Come up as you used to do, but for heaven's sake don't let Irene wander round the village any more.'

This would have been manna to Jenny a day before since it would have given her a chance to see Benedict. Now she was not going to bother about Benedict any more. However she was fond of Irene and liked her toys and she liked Uncle Edward to show her books. So she murmured dignified thanks. Then Helena left, inviting them all to coffee after dinner.

In the end Mr and Mrs Owen stayed to clear up, and Jenny, Alan and the doctor walked up to The Hollies. Nobody held Jenny's hand this time. She had the impression that the doctor was a rather quiet sort of man and had taken her hand only in the stress of the moment. That in a way made his gesture more delightful.

Irene was sitting on her mother's knee and looked pale but not frightened. She seemed glad to see Jenny and said, 'I've got two new puzzles. And the ghosts in the Iron House are kind and you needn't be afraid.' Uncle Edward looked rather tired after the upset of the previous day, but he made his usual comic remark. 'What did your gran say to you running up and down the road in your night things?'

'She was asleep,' Jenny said still very restrained.

'A good thing. She might have had a fit,' Uncle Edward said; and then 'I suppose you ought to have a reward. A picture book of plants?'

'No thank you,' Jenny said. 'I'm not going to be a plant woman any longer. I'm going to be a vet.' She saw the doctor look up and was glad.

'A book on animals' insides then?'

But Jenny, still feeling noble after Helena's apology, decided still to be saintly. She remembered Crabby who had told her that he had nowhere to go and wanted a job. So she said, 'You know Crabby – Steve really – at Meadow Grange. He wants to be a gardener. Could you help him?'

Uncle Edward asked, 'How old is he?'

'Sixteen next week,' Jenny said. She was going to give him a present of a pot of honey because he was studying bees.

'We were thinking of finding somebody to do a bit of weeding,' Uncle Edward said. He cocked an eye at Jos who gave a little nod. 'Tell him to come up and see us one morning,' Edward said.

And the blessed doctor said, 'Jenny will be getting a halo soon.'

He and Alan left soon afterwards. The doctor's smart car stood in front of the shop and Mr and Mrs Owen stood at the door to see them off. The doctor thanked them and got in, and Jenny went round to the driver's side and said, 'Will you come again?' Alan, beside the doctor, laughed. 'She's always adoring somebody,' and one of those frightful blushes that were beginning to plague Jenny came all over her face. But the doctor said in his quiet godlike way, 'I might if I were asked.'

Jenny told her school friends that Dr Gregg was the best doctor in London, and he was handsomer than any man on television. And he liked her and was going to help her to be a vet.

'You could a' knocked me down with a feather,' Mrs Noakes said. The nurse had again installed her with Anna in the small room by the door of the home.

But she was a different Mrs Noakes. She looked younger and the droop had gone. She was almost the old cheerful gossip that Anna had known by the railway arch.

She began talking almost before the nurse had shut the door. She waved a paper and said, 'My Ted's come back.'

'Your Ted?'

'You know dear. The gentleman who used to come and see me in our pub before the war. Him with beautiful manners. And then he found me when I was knocked out in an air-raid.'

She held up a letter. It said, 'With best wishes from Edward Carey. I hope you are more comfortable now.'

'He's sent me a lovely box of chocolates,' Mrs Noakes said. 'And there's a PS on the back of his letter about him sending other gifts. The old dames here think it's a lovely romance.'

Anna remembered the talk at Ladyhill. She said, 'But this is from Edward Carey.'

'Yes dear. That was his name. He don't say what he's been doing since the war. He's retired by now, I expect.'

'But this is Edward Carey from Worcestershire.'

'Yes dear. My Ted always did move about.' She looked beaming at Anna. 'I wonder how he found where I was. Dr Gregg, I expect.'

The chocolates had done more than make her happy. 'Some of them here,' she told Anna, 'ain't bad old girls. When the chocs came we was all in the sitting-room and Miss Mossop, who makes rude remarks about pubs and is always talking about her vicar, was telling how the blessed man had called on her and her mother and brought a box of peppermints because they'd helped in some bazaar. "A nice friend like that leaves happy memories," she says in her lah-di-dah way, just as if none of us has had nice friends.

'And at that moment the nurse brought in Ted's parcel. She unwrapped it for me as my eyes aren't good and read the message, and everybody watched and said, "Who's it from?" And I said, "A nice friend but not a vicar," and that made them curious.

'I didn't bear them no malice. I was so pleased that my Ted had found me. And I took the chocs round, and it was a big box, and everybody had one. And then Miss Mossop had to shut up, and I told them about my Ted and the air-raid. And now they're always asking me for stories, and they say I'm better than the telly.'

There seemed nothing that Anna could say. She thought, 'I'll tell Edward to write.' Meanwhile Mrs Noakes went on to tell her that some of the old ladies now offered to take her out to sit in the garden. Relationships had certainly sweetened, for another old lady looked in to accompany Mrs Noakes to tea.

The next day Anna telephoned to Edward. It was a three-sided conversation, as her mother happened to be there. Anna talked to Edward and he passed the news on.

He was at first amused and then perturbed when Anna told him that he had become 'Ted'. 'Will you write and undeceive her?' Anna said, but he asked how could he, an unknown man living miles from London, explain why he had begun to send her presents? Anna asked what was the alternative.

Then Mrs Dean came to the telephone. How old was Mrs Noakes?

'Over seventy, I think.'

'Is it absolutely necessary to start explaining? Edward's far away.'

'Isn't it rather mean to play-act with her?'

'One has to do an awful lot of play-acting in life,' Mrs Dean said. She had always been successful in work with committees. 'I'll ask Edward.'

Edward came back to the telephone. 'I'm like you, Anna. I don't want any play-acting. But if it makes the old lady happy . . .'

'Let's leave it for the time being then,' Anna said. She thought of the change in Mrs Noakes. It would be too bad to spoil it. She must ask Tristram, she thought, what he would have done.

When she next visited the home Mrs Noakes had received a beautiful bottle of eau-do-cologne.

The Deans were opening letters in an Edinburgh hotel lounge. They were half way through a family motoring holiday, mainly arranged for the benefit of Hughie who had become more important since his escapade with Carol. He had also, oddly, begun to earn a little money.

The Warburton discussions were over. The firm had agreed that there was not really enough for Hughie to do. Dad had suggested that he should come at once into the family works. But no. Hughie had had enough of factories for the moment. So it had been arranged that he should attend an engineering course in the autumn.

But meanwhile Hughie had become a car-mender. It had begun when he had gone out to tinker with the Carey car while his mother talked to Edward. The car had gone so much better afterwards that Edward had mentioned Hughie to a farmer who was complaining that there was no garage in Ladyhill. The farmer had been pleased, and so Hughie had gone on. He had begun to service cars for some of Dad's acquaintances in Birmingham.

So now to oblige him they had motored north with Hughie driving half the time. They had concentrated on engineering works – Rolls Royce, the railway museum at York, Newcastle's famous bridge. Now they were heading for the Scottish railway bridges. Mrs Dean had brought a pile of books, which she shared with Anna, for, she said, 'a little light relief'.

She had arranged for letters to be sent on by the family help. Anna, of course, had none, and the sense of absence from Tristram deepened.

She had not seen him for eleven days. But she still had not mentioned his name to her family.

Mrs Dean was turning over the envelopes, and she picked on one addressed in an old-fashioned flowing hand. She frowned, read the letter again, and then said to Hughie, 'I suppose you'd better know. Carol has disappeared.'

Hughie had been reading letters of his own as he stood by the door. He dropped them, stooped to pick them up and emerged with a red face. He frowned on his mother in a new way and said loudly, 'Who says so?'

'Mrs Cole, the woman with the home for girls.'

'Damn the home for girls,' Hughie said with uncharacteristic violence.

'It may be a damned home,' Mrs Dean said with her usual touch of sharpness, 'but it did take Carol at a moment's notice.'

'And Carol didn't like it.'

Mrs Dean glanced through the letter again. 'Not Mrs Cole's fault. The other girls didn't like Carol. They had an argument one evening and the next morning she packed her bag and left without giving an address.'

Hughie thrust his letters into his pocket and turned to the door. Anna had a sudden fear and asked, 'You haven't had anything to do with this?'

'Wish I had,' he said defiantly.

'You haven't been seeing her?' Anna had forgotten her resolution not to dictate.

But he was a new Hughie. 'It's none of your business.' Then the old docile Hughie returned for a moment. 'I tried to see her if you want to know, but she wouldn't.'

'Be sensible,' Mrs Dean said gently. But he had gone; opened the door and galloped down the stairs.

It was then that Anna saw him for the first time not as her 'little brother' but as an adult suffering as she was suffering. 'I'll go and look for him,' she said and followed down the stairs though Dad called after her, 'Don't go out. It's raining.'

But Hughie must have fled into the street. She stood at the hotel door looking out and thinking how often she had seen a street like this, wet with lights, when she had come out of cafés with Tristram. And her sense of his absence grew. He was hundreds of miles away but at least she would see him again, while Hughie had no hope of seeing Carol.

He came in at last with the shoulders of his jacket glistening with rain. He saw her and tried to escape, bounding up the stairs to his bedroom. But she followed him and caught him up as he fumbled with his key. He opened the door and she walked in too.

Why had she followed? To console him she thought, but the conversation developed differently. She began, 'Hughie, you'll have to look after the family in future,' and when he said roughly, 'Don't know what you mean,' said 'I shall never marry.'

He was much taller now than she, and a great desire came over her to confide in him. He said, 'Of course you'll marry if you want to. You and your doctor . . .'

'He's not my doctor, and he's got nothing to do with it.'

'But Mother thinks . . .'

'Mother's wrong.'

It was like a flood – the desire to talk at last. And there he stood, for the first time a big brother. She said, 'What would you do if you loved somebody who hadn't the ordinary feelings?'

'Give him up, I suppose.'

'Impossible. I couldn't possibly.'

He looked down on her surprised. She remembered how he had seemed in Carol's power, but here he was back, and she was glad. 'Why do you ask *me*?' he said.

'Only because we're sister and brother and we're both upset. But never mind.'

But he had grown up. He did not dodge away. He asked, 'Have you told him what you feel?'

'No need. He knows.'

'Wouldn't it be an idea to talk things over with him?'

He was right, of course. She had never looked squarely at this Tristram affair; only gone home and suffered in private. It was an idiotic way to behave. One should use judgment; be in control. She was suddenly strong, looking at her life. She would cease to drift. She would talk to Tristram and compel some response.

Now she said to Hughie, 'I think you're right. I must do something.' And then, 'Thanks very much. You're a great help.'

The surprise on his face deepened. Then he was beaming.

'I never knew that you would want to talk like this.'

'But I do. I've been making a fool of myself too.'

'I'm glad I'm not the only one. I suppose we shall just have to peg on.'

He took off his wet jacket and got a towel to rub his wet hair.

'Come on. We'd better go down to the other two.' It was the first occasion that he had ever directed her.

She thought at the time that that conversation had changed both their lives. But afterwards it appeared that it had changed only his. He had grown up, but she was still a slave.

She returned to London in a mood of determination. She would talk to Tristram; say, 'We can't go on in the same way for ever.' But first, when she saw him standing waiting, she allowed herself a moment of pure joy. They had been hundreds of miles apart and now they were back again. She said, 'Good. Oh good.'

And then she could not embark on serious discussion at once. She must talk about her holiday. She said, in the midst of a description of the Highlands, 'Hughie's different now. We've followed your advice.'

'What advice?' he asked vaguely.

That was the first check. He did not even remember the words that she had treasured. And there was something worse. She asked, 'Where have *you* been? Only London?'

'I had a trip to Bristol.'

'Friends?'

'A BBC job.'

'You mean you'd go away?'

'Apparently not. My natural history was defective. I didn't know enough about foxes.'

So while she had been thinking of him all the time he had blithely planned his disappearance. It was all very well to decide on a serious discussion on love, but now there was nothing to found a discussion on. She sat back listening to the noises round her and thinking, 'It's all an illusion. I have nothing.'

He knew, of course, that he had hurt her. He was sensitive to her feelings even while he disregarded them. He said as an apology, 'I probably shan't look for a job outside again. I don't particularly want to leave London.' But she was still prostrate and did not answer.

It might have been a disastrous meeting, but it was not. He knew that she was curious about his life, and he began to talk. 'You asked what I've been doing. I've been sorting my father's papers.'

She was his slave. She roused herself and asked, 'Did you find anything interesting?'

'He began well,' Tristram said, and went on talking, still apparently as an apology. Perhaps as an explanation too. He knew that he did not behave like ordinary people. He told how his father had just left Oxford with a history degree and had joined the Ministry of Education when, on a holiday in North Wales, he met the young teacher Bronwen. For a week they discussed Welsh history and literature, and when he left he was in love. He went on writing to her and spent all his holidays in Wales and proposed marriage several times. Both families were against the union and so was she for a long time. 'But my father was quietly persistent,' Tristram said.

The Welsh girl had never been to London, so he had taken a house in Hampstead to give her some open spaces. The beginning of the marriage might have been happy, but they had been less than two years together and Tristram was a baby when war broke out. He and his mother were evacuated to Wales and stayed for nearly six years.

Tristram remembered a white-bearded grandfather who had also been a teacher, but he died before the end of the war. The boy was old enough before they left to have learned a little Welsh, and he remembered rushing streams, clouds on the heights, sheep and wet slates. London, he said, was like a foreign country when they returned.

His father who had come out when he could – but it had been seldom – was a stranger. 'His voice was different from the voices I was used to, and he did not know how to treat me. He had got used to living alone.

'My mother could not bear London. She could have done more to share my father's life, but she developed asthma or something like it quite soon. She seemed never well. I remember her sitting in her room with an inhaler and working on translations of Welsh poems. She did not write badly. Sometimes she spoke to me in Welsh, which my father did not understand. She didn't go with my father to any Civil Service functions. Her health was the excuse. There were no quarrels. He gave way to her and spent longer and longer hours at his office. I think he had other women friends.

'I never felt easy at school. My speech was different. They called me Jasmine. I think the only amusements I had came from my two aunts, my father's sisters, who lived near us. My aunt Margaret took me to the theatre and Tower of London and museums. I didn't tell the boys at school. The would have laughed still more.'

When he was thirteen his father had sent him to school in Switzerland. 'It was a travelled family, and I think that he wanted to get me away from the home atmosphere. My mother didn't object. I imagine she felt guilty, and she thought that I should enjoy the mountains. I did, but I missed her.'

His mother had died when he was sixteen and still in Switzerland. His father told him that there was no need to return. When he got home for the holidays the house was different. 'Somehow free-er and brighter, but my mother's large photograph of Snowdon had been left in her room. Her death was probably a relief to my father and yet he mourned her. My aunts came in quite a lot. They are excellent women.'

It was strange how all this came pouring out. Tristram had told Anna almost nothing before, but he was good at talking and he obviously realised that he had offended her. Gradually Anna lost the feeling of disaster and began to ask questions, flattered that he should have told her so much. Their meetings seemed often like this – repulse and then some offering.

'What has happened since?'

'Not much. After Switzerland I stayed with my father and took a London degree. He seemed peaceful enough with a few Civil Service friends, his books and local societies. He didn't talk much to me and didn't seem to need me. When I said I wanted to hear French again he let me go back – to the Sorbonne.'

'But you returned in the end.'

'We were both getting older.'

She was to wonder afterwards where he had found all his friends. He seemed to make friends everywhere with his curious lack of convention and habit of asking unexpected questions. She often saw his effect on people in the cafés.

'And now?' she asked.

'Qui sait? I'm going to be bored by taking two evening classes in French in a week or two.'

'And your writing?'

He did not answer. They had already stayed well over their usual hour and she did not insist. When they parted she was relaxed, enriched. It was of Tristram rather than of herself that she was thinking. The discussion about her own feelings could wait.

Helena and Jos sat on their bed at the end of a busy day. The house was quiet, Helena had peered in at Irene to see that she was asleep.

Millie, the house's earliest riser, had gone up to her room an hour before. Edward had as usual paused at their door to say goodnight and limped off to his room across the landing. Now there was bright autumn moonlight outside and, inside, darkness and warmth from the day's living.

The two often paused at this time to talk of the events of the day. They were too busy, he with his pottery and the gardens and she with another book and Irene, to meet much before bedtime. And now, since the incident of the Iron House, Irene had taken more of Helena's time.

To everyone's surprise, Irene seemed to have suffered little from her adventure. The ghosts that had come, she said, had been kind and there was no need to be afraid of anything. She fell asleep more quickly in the evening and did not call out so much.

She had had the extra stress in early September of beginning school. But, after one or two mornings when she did not want her breakfast, she walked off quite happily with Helena and came back with pages of letters and numbers. She was small for her age and one of the smallest girls in the school, and her family was respected in the village, and the big girls made a pet of her. She had begun already to draw their portraits. The girls took them home and this made Irene popular.

It was Helena who had suffered. Ever since the death of the Polish soldier, whom she had loved at the end of the war twenty years before, she had been afraid of disasters, and now Irene's adventure had revived the old fears.

She insisted on taking the child to school and calling for her morning and afternoon. She would want to be told everything that the child had done during the day, and the two would return talking earnestly until Irene said, 'That's all. There's nothing any more.'

That afternoon Irene had come back with a mark on her forehead where a chestnut had hit her during a conker fight between two boys, and Helena was pale with anxiety. 'An inch further and it would have been in her eye.'

Now Helena said as they sat on the bed, 'I know I'm being a fool. I must fight against it. But I can't help some of it. I'm always dreaming that Irene's being murdered or falling over cliffs.'

Jos asked, 'Do you think it's good for Irene to be so fussed after?' and then wished he had not, for that set off another anxiety. 'Perhaps I'm ruining her life.'

'Oh, for heaven's sake,' Jos said. 'You know you aren't.'

Long before, when they had been only acquaintances, they had had a long discussion on Benedict, then a rebellious fourteen-year-old. Jos had told her not to be so tragic about him; to 'treat him more lightly'. She had followed his advice and the tension had eased, and now Benedict had distinguished himself at Cambridge and when he came home he and Helena enjoyed long caustic arguments. But instead Helena was agonising over Irene.

Helena had wanted another child to keep Irene company, but none had come. 'I'd have been better with half-a-dozen offspring,' she said now. 'I could have dissipated my nightmares then.'

Jos had become her chief soother. He said that she made him feel sensible in a way he had never felt before. Now he encouraged her. 'We may manage it yet.'

'I don't think so. It's too late. What an idiotic world it is – we waiting in vain for another child and millions of other children wanting homes.'

'You've been talking to Agnes Dean.'

'I have. But I also remember my old war-time nursery. Some of those babies had nobody. Heaven knows what became of them.'

'You'll be worn out tomorrow if you sit up making speeches.'

'Blow tomorrow. Jos, if we did come across a child that needed a home . . .'

'Bad nights, nappy-washing, messes, teething,' he said not quite joking.

'Would you really hate an orphan child?'

'I expect so.'

'Then I won't think of it. Only it seems a waste when we have a comfortable home and a lonely little girl. Never mind, I'll go and have a bath.'

He became serious. 'Do what you like. I'm all right if I have you and Irene.'

'But you'd be horrible to a new child.'

'You know I wouldn't. But I might compare it with Irene.'

'But not bash it on the head.'

'I'd leave you to do that.'

She went to the window to pull the curtains and stood looking out at the moonlight. 'It's a beautiful night. Sometimes I think I'll run away from the lot of you and worship God in the desert.'

'Tell the authorities that and they'll give you a child at once.'

She turned and made a grimace at him. 'It's strange that such a mild man should have such a sharp tongue.' Then she pulled the curtains and their conversation ended, as if often did, in laughter.

It took a long time to persuade Edward to visit the Garden Home, but in the end it seemed necessary if Mrs Noakes was to be kept happy. As the whole venture of sending weekly gifts had been to make her happy it was unreasonable, Anna thought, to refuse this last service. Mrs Dean sympathised with Edward in his unwillingness to show himself, but in the end, as Mrs Noakes's pleading continued, she thought he should give way.

Through the summer Edward had sent parcels. Millie, who had once had a mother-in-law living with her, advised on the choice. He had sent sweets and perfume, soap and handkerchiefs. Many of his gifts had been able to be shared, so that Mrs Noakes would remain popular with the other residents.

But then Mrs Noakes began to ask questions. She wanted to know what Ted had done since the war. Anna found it easiest to supply details from Edward's own life. She said that Ted was living with a sister in the country. He had never married. Yes, he was quite well off. He gardened a lot, but he had a rheumatic knee. Then Mrs Noakes asked how Anna had got to know Ted. It was easy to say that Anna's family lived near him in the Midlands. But Mrs Noakes knew that Anna went home each month. Was it a simple journey, and if so, did Ted ever come to London?

Anna said Ted's rheumatic knee kept him at home, but Mrs Noakes thought that he could sit in a train, couldn't he? And if he was well off he could afford a car to meet him at the station. If he was fond enough of her to send the presents surely he could come just once.

'You'd better kill me off,' Edward said when they consulted.

'That would upset her terribly,' Anna said.

After a time Mrs Noakes began to suspect some mystery. She imagined various lurid reasons why Edward would not come to London. Had Ted really a wife who was jealous? Had he committed some crime and had to hide in the country? Had he had some terrible accident and was deformed?

The residents joined in the suggestions. Was Ted really as fond of Mrs Noakes as she claimed? Was he not as wealthy as he seemed?

Every time that a parcel arrived they asked, 'Is he coming?' Anna grew quite to dread the questions.

Edward, supported by The Hollies family, resisted till early October. Seeing him worried, Helena suggested that he should write to Dr Gregg, as he was the doctor at the home. The doctor replied that Anna knew Mrs Noakes better than he did and Edward should be guided by her. But, if Edward did think of coming, he, Dr Gregg, would meet him and take him to the home.

The doctor's letter eased Helena's anxiety. After all he had been marvellous when Irene was found. Mrs Dean said that, if the deed was decent, it was better to do than not to do. Anna said that if he came it would be a burden off her shoulders and she would be at the home if Edward liked. Edward at last wrote unwillingly that he would come.

He regretted it, of course, on that Saturday morning. He had hardly slept, and then there was all the fuss of putting on gentlemanly clothes and having an early breakfast. Jos drove him into Birmingham, and they talked of the work to be done in the garden, and Edward thought that Jos would be returning in peace while he . . . He did not even know if he would go on playing Ted or confess. In either case he would be deeply embarrassed.

In the train his mind unexpectedly went to Rose. She had been a great comfort, and he wished she were with him now. But he had sent her away to Yorkshire, and she had settled down, as she would do anywhere, but he was not sure now whether it had been the right thing. He knew that she missed him, and she had left him with Mrs Dean – a wise experienced woman but without Rose's sweetness. And the Deans had got him into this trouble. Rose would somehow have arranged things better.

The morning was dull and the London suburbs seemed everlasting. But Dr Gregg was waiting at Euston – tall, rather silent but reliable. He seemed pleased when Edward told him that Anna would be at the home. The doctor thought her unusual – mixing social work with journalism. 'She seems to be a girl of drive and determination.'

'Like her mother,' Edward said, and he mentally apologised for his criticism in the train. He really enjoyed Agnes Dean's visits very much.

He cheered up a little over lunch. The doctor offered him a meal in a quiet expensive place, and he was interested in Ladyfield. Edward talked of the history of his house, The Hollies, how his grandfather had built it on a field and begun the gardens and orchard, and how his aunt, the retired schoolmistress, had added to them. Edward was pleased at the doctor's interest and he described how, when he had been teaching in London in his twenties, his aunt had left him the house and he had gone out there and felt the pleasure of owning and cultivating land. The doctor said, 'And I on the contrary live on a street corner without a garden,' and Edward felt his own good fortune.

But two o'clock came, and they had to move on. Then Edward had a moment of despair. He did not know what was going to happen but whatever it was he was quite unable to cope with it. He sat in the car with closed eyes. At home he would have been in his chair and having a short afternoon sleep which divided up the day. Now he was going to meet an old woman whom he did not know and pretend to be somebody he was not. He said to the doctor, 'I don't know how you can bear to live here.'

And then it seemed that he might escape after all. When the big door of the home was opened the matron was there. She said to the doctor 'We've been trying to get you. Mrs Noakes has had a stroke.'

It seemed to be the effect of excitement, the matron said. All the week she had been talking of Ted. And then, getting up from breakfast that morning, she had fallen and now was half paralysed though she could still speak a little. 'She's had a hard life and been kept going by her spirit. But she's really very frail. We've put her in a room on her own.'

And Edward, to his shame, felt a sudden hope. 'I don't want to upset her any more,' he said.

The matron smiled on him. Apparently she did not know of his deceit. 'She has very happy memories of you, Mr Carey. And now that you've come so far . . . It would be a pity if she didn't have a glimpse of you. But we'll see what Dr Gregg thinks.'

And it seemed that Dr Gregg put his patients above his friends, and he decided in favour of Mrs Noakes even though he knew of Edward's unwillingness. Edward was given a chair in the hall while doctor and matron went upstairs. He sat uneasily conscious of many curious eyes from the large sitting-room. The residents watched like cats. There they all were, cooped up in a world away from the air and without enough to think about. He was embarrassed as well as sleepy.

Then the doctor and matron came down slowly. The matron said, 'She's still asking for you, Mr Carey. Miss Dean is there.' And the doctor had only a little mercy. 'No need to stay more than a few minutes.'

The doctor helped him up and he followed the matron up the stairs. She opened a door, said 'Just say a few words to her' and vanished.

Edward hesitated in the doorway. The room smelt of eau-de-cologne, possibly from his own gift. Anna sat by the window and gave him a half smile. A buxom nurse came forward and there in the bed were a grey-white patch of hair and a ridge almost too small to be a human body.

And suddenly all Edward's embarrassment left him. Here was something beyond embarrassment – a human creature wanting his help. Whether he was Ted or not did not matter. He felt a great pity, and went to the bed, and the patch of hair turned and a small pointed face with red blinking eyes looked up. A thin arm with a veined hand came out feeling for him. He took the hand, and a small hoarse voice said, 'You're a bigger man than I remember, dear.' He was Ted to her and she had his hand, and that was what she wanted.

She muttered something inaudible; then the hoarse voice said, 'I do like them things that you send' and then, with a touch of joie-de-vivre, 'Them with rum fillings – lovely chocs.'

The nurse brought a chair, and Edward's stick clattered to the floor.

At the sound Mrs Noakes opened her eyes again. 'It's been a long time, Ted, but you been good and come at last.' Her eyes shut but she still held Edward's hand.

He sat for a quarter of an hour in the quiet room. Anna and the nurse, sitting by the window, occasionally made a low-voiced remark. But it did not destroy the peace, and Edward by the bed meditated on memory.

Why was one not more astonished at memory? Here was a sick woman taking comfort in holding his hand because of memories of more than twenty years before. And no-one knew how many memories he had within him. Something, thought to be forgotten, would flash up suddenly. Who could say what memories were in that thin ridge in the bed?

Perhaps memories were the one part of us that remained. And if so, if so . . . The hand holding his loosed its grasp and slid away, and he had no time to think any more. The nurse came and picked up his stick. He was very stiff and he had lost the thread of his meditation, but a feeling of peace remained. It was partly that the ordeal was over and partly that he had been somewhere deeper than the ordinary run of experience. The nurse helped him up and said, 'I think you can go now,' and Anna came and took his arm. She looked solemn, but he wanted to say to her, 'It's all right. Our memories remain.'

They left soon afterwards. The doctor went up once again, and Edward and Anna were given cups of tea in the hall. Fortunately the line of chairs in the big sitting-room was empty, as the residents had gone to tea. For ten minutes Edward and Anna talked of trifles, and then the doctor returned and said, 'No point in staying any longer.'

Edward watched Anna with the doctor. Mrs Dean had thought there was some romance between them, but they seemed merely friendly. The doctor politely invited Anna to come and see Edward off at Euston, but she said, 'Thankyou, but I've a pile of weekend work. If you'd just drop me at a bus-stop. I'll ring Ladyhill to say that Edward's on his way.'

The doctor drove her all the way to her flat, and there was no time for more talk. The car headed north for Euston and arrived only a quarter of an hour before the Birmingham train left. Edward would have liked to talk more to Dr Gregg, but there was only time to say thankyou. 'Have a good journey,' the doctor said cheerfully. Somehow Mrs Noakes had dropped out of their thoughts.

But she returned to Edward in the train. He lay back and felt again the old hand in his. He had thought at the time, 'We are all founts of memories', but there had been no time for a conclusion. Now he must think. But instead he fell comfortably asleep and did not wake till the lights of Birmingham were spread below. He woke feeling that something significant had happened though he did not quite know what.

Jos was waiting for him. 'Have you had an awful day?'

'No,' Edward said. 'Interesting.'

Two days later Anna telephoned that Mrs Noakes had died.

Now Anna had no longer to visit the Garden Home, and she had a feeling of release. It was the busy season in London, and she was out attending meetings or exhibitions on most days. But she would have time to do some reading in the evenings, she thought. Tristram was lending her French books.

But it was only a few days after Mrs Noakes's death that the telephone rang. She had only just returned from work, and when she heard the doctor's voice she said, a little irritated, 'Can you wait? I've just got in.' Then she heard something howling, and asked, 'Whatever's that?'

'A baby. Carol's left it.'

'*What*? Has she come back? All right. I won't be a minute.'

She flung on her coat again, and ran through the wet streets. The surgery door was still open though patients and receptionist had gone. Laurence was in his consulting room walking up and down with a howling bundle. He looked relieved when he saw Anna. 'Carol timed it well – just when my last patient had departed.'

The baby yelled in a paroxysm of fury. 'Here, give it to me,' Anna said. She knew a little about handling infants from married Birmingham friends. Laurence passed the bundle over, and she began walking with it, but it howled more loudly than ever. 'It's hungry,' she said, already with an air of possession.

A carry-cot was on the doctor's table. It had old bits of blanket at the bottom, but on top was a carton of baby food with a feeding bottle. Anna said, 'We'd better try some,' and Laurence took the carton and bottle to his kitchen behind. The bundle was very wet and Anna laid it on the table and unwrapped it. She found a mass of black hair, blue eyes, a red face and wide mouth. There were two napkins in the carry-cot, and rather clumsily she pinned them on. She called to Laurence above the howling, 'It's a girl.'

He came with the bottle, and Anna sat and fed the child. It sucked greedily, brought up wind and sucked again. There was a blessed silence.

Laurence began to apologise. 'I wouldn't have bothered you but I thought you should be consulted as it is Carol's.' He told how the surgery had just finished when there had been a long peal at the bell. He had gone out and found the carry-cot on the steps, and a moment later had heard a car round the corner whirr away. 'She must have been watching to see that I came,' he said. 'She can't be wholly irresponsible.'

A rough piece of paper with bold black writing lay in the carry-cot. It said, with some spelling mistakes, 'Please be good to her. She's six days old. I have a new boyfriend who has seen me through, and we are going abroad and you won't see me again.'

The baby had finished the bottle and was asleep. It was warm now though it was dressed in only an old faded blue coat too large for it. Anna sat feeling a vague pleasure in the sleeping bundle. Her mother had said that she had been good with Hughie when he was a baby, and she supposed that she had some maternal instinct. This was becoming her baby. She said, 'What shall we do with her?'

'It will have to go to the babies' home for the present.'

'Oh no. Carol hated homes.'

Anna With Tristram

'What's the alternative?'

Anna wondered wildly if she could say, 'I'll take her.' But of course it was impossible. She had to earn a living and there were no facilities at her flat. She asked, 'Couldn't one of your receptionists or your nurse take her?'

'They're busy women. They might have it for a night, but they couldn't keep it. It's better for the child to go straight to a home and not be moved about. We can discuss its future later.'

He was right, of course, and yet Anna felt indignant. He was going to give their baby to some big official home with red tape and smart uncaring nurses. At the same time she knew that she was being foolish to object.

And she could not help admiring the way he approached the home with authority and a calm explanation. After a few minutes he put the telephone down and said, 'They'll take it. I'll complete the arrangements in the morning. They'll try to find Carol of course.'

She wanted to ask what kind of life this child would have with Carol, but she was aware that she must not get too closely involved. But when Laurence said, 'Perhaps you'll put it back in the carry-cot,' she objected. 'The carry-cot is none too clean – and cold. I'll carry her. Have you got any kind of wrapping?'

He went to the kitchen and brought out an old cardigan, and then shouted up to Jack that he would be out for a short time. Outside it was raining, and Anna held the child closely to her.

It was over very quickly. The home, a big red house, was near and the door was opened promptly by a young nurse. Anna handed over the baby and Laurence the carry-cot and Laurence said, 'I'll be in touch with you in the morning.' Then he drove Anna back to her flat, said 'You'd better have something to eat' and drove away.

Anna went in troubled – partly for the baby and partly for herself – that strong maternal feeling that had seized her as she held it. She rang up her mother but did not mention her feelings, and Mrs Dean made two comments. The first was, 'Carol must have thought highly of Dr Gregg to have left the baby with him,' and the second was, 'What about the Merediths?'

It was six weeks later, and four of them stood round the cot, Anna and the doctor on one side and Helena and Jos Meredith on the other. During the weeks the authorities had been trying to trace Carol, but she had been too clever for them. She had gone.

During that time the baby had changed. The black mop of hair had gone and a red fuzz was beginning. The eyes had altered from blue to hazel, and the red face had grown pale. The baby was not pretty, with a small snub nose and wide mouth, but she was large and, the nurses said, took her food well.

Her behaviour had changed too. She lay quietly staring at nothing, only once or twice giving a small cry and looking towards Anna. For Anna had become half a substitute parent.

She had been going two or three times a week to see Cindy, as the nurses called the child (short for Cinderella). She had rung up the home without telling the doctor, and the matron had invited her to call. She went in the evening and stayed for half an hour in the room with its eight cots of infants waiting for parents. 'Have her out, Miss Dean,' the nurses said, and they talked of the blight that falls on infants who form no bond with adults. They become listless, uninterested, making no demands, and this was happening with Cindy.

On those evenings Anna nursed the baby and played with her plump hands. The child had begun to know her and become restless when she appeared. And each time Anna had hated putting her back into the cot and leaving her.

Early she had rung up the doctor and suggested that he should contact Helena Meredith. Anna was already jealous of a future mother, but of course the baby's welfare must come first. Later the doctor had rung back to say that the Merediths were interested, and then she told him that she was visiting the home. He praised her highly, saying that she was probably making a future adoption easier. 'You really are an unselfish girl, Miss Dean.' She did not confess that it was not unselfishness at all but the feeling that the child was hers.

She had thought Laurence himself cold in his attitude to the baby, but he had immediately begun correspondence with the Merediths, and now that they had come to look at Cindy he had come too. So the four stood round the cot and the baby made her usual small cry when she saw Anna, but Anna now might not pick her up.

A nurse came forward and said, 'Have her out Mrs Meredith,' as she had said to Anna. So Helena stooped and lifted the baby, and Anna noticed that she was practised in the way of holding infants, bringing the baby up to her shoulder with a supporting hand. Cindy was quiet, but she looked across at Anna.

Helena began to walk the child up and down, and they all watched. Jos said to the nurse, 'She looks quite intelligent.'

'Oh, she's all there,' the nurse said. The doctor commented quietly to Anna, 'It looks as if it's going to be all right,' but she was feeling her arms empty, and said nothing.

Helena came back with the baby and put her into Jos's arms. He said, 'What a weight! Is she going to be our second artist?'

'Of course not,' Helena said. 'She's going to be a boxer. But she weighs twice as much as Irene did at her age.' And Anna heard the voice of a mother bent on finding some special quality in her child.

Jos put the baby back into the cot and she began to whimper. Helena said to Anna, 'Do you think you could hold her while we decide?' And for a moment Anna's empty arms were filled again and she began to play with Cindy in the usual way and the baby stopped crying. She had got into the habit of putting a hand to Anna's lips for Anna gently to blow on it, and she made this gesture now. And Anna thought, 'It's ridiculous. She really is my child.'

Helena and Jos were looking questioningly at one another. Helena said, 'What do you think?' and he answered, 'What do *you* think?" And Helena said, 'There's a three-month probation period. We have a way out if it doesn't work.'

The nurse asked, 'You mean you want to take her now?'

'It might be the best thing,' Helena said, and the nurse agreed. 'The sooner she's settled the better,' and Anna stood and listened, while the baby patted her lips.

'I'll go and phone Edward,' Helena said. 'After all it's his house.' She went away and for the last time Anna had the baby to herself. The doctor and Jos began to talk by the empty cot.

The doctor seemed to be telling Jos how she, Anna, had been visiting the baby regularly, and Jos was saying that she was like her own mother – useful. But Anna moved away and took Cindy a tour of the other cots in the room which the child was soon to leave. She whispered, 'You'll forget me of course.'

Helena returned smiling. 'Joking as usual,' she said. 'He says the baby had better come at once so that she can have a Christmas party. He brought Irene to the phone, and she would like the baby to sleep in her room.'

'So . . . .' Jos said.

'Are you sure, Jos?'

'We can hardly back out now,' he said.

Then the matron came in with papers – the child's age and weight, details of when she entered the home, instruction on food – and said she would inform the authorities. She did not anticipate any difficulties since the Merediths had a comfortable home and were friends of Dr Gregg, but a social worker would come to inspect their house. A nurse came and took Cindy from Anna's arms. 'She'd better have her feed if she's going to travel.' There was talk of equipment. The home would provide a shawl and the garments that Cindy was wearing, and Helena said that they would be home in time to shop, and in any case she had Irene's old equipment. All this time Anna stood on one side, her arms empty, and finally Helena noticed and turned to her. 'You must come and see her at Christmas. Laurence says you've been awfully good.'

It was nice of Helena, but the sense of loss remained. Anna did not hold the baby again. The nurse brought her back wrapped in the shawl and put her into Helena's arms. The baby was quiet after her feed, and the four visitors with the matron went down the stairs. The car was near. Helena settled beside Jos in the front seat. They waved and were gone.

The matron said to Anna, 'I expect you'll quite miss your visits here.'

But it was not the end of that gloomy day.

The matron went in and Dr Gregg and Anna moved to his car. It was still early afternoon, and Laurence said, 'You must have some lunch.' Anna would have preferred to return to her flat and think over the loss of the baby, but they had been allies in the care of Cindy and she could not refuse.

She was used to drifting into any kind of café with Tristram, but Laurence drove over the bridge to a hotel and wanted her to have a full lunch. But they were late and the dining-room was only half full and she persuaded him to order only coffee and sandwiches.

Yet he seemed to want to spin the meal out as long as possible. She had the feeling that he was preparing to make some statement and had to summon up courage. He talked on about nothings – wondering how long it would take the Merediths to reach home, announcing that he had found another old lady to fill Mrs Noakes's place at the home. Anna, melancholy with the loss of Cindy, wished he would stop, and several times said, 'Oughtn't you to get back?'

though it was Saturday. That made him hesitate, but he began again.

At the end she had an inkling of what he wanted to say, and she grew nervous. Finally she said, 'I really must go,' and he stopped short. He had not said what he had intended to say and she hoped she could escape it, but tension grew as they drove back over the bridge. She tried to fill the silence with desultory remarks – how the colour of the river changed with the sky; how it must be difficult for seagulls to find enough food. He did not answer, and she did not know if he was concentrating on the traffic or nerving himself for this statement that would not come.

He drove to her flat and she got out quickly and thought that she was free. But he followed and stood over her and she was trapped. Then at last the statement came. 'You're good with babies. You ought to have some of your own.'

It was an innocuous remark, but she knew what it meant. It was typical of him that he should talk of her rather than of himself. She saw his big hand in the dusk approach hers and then drop again. She said, 'Oh please don't.'

But he had begun and he wanted to finish. 'We've done several things together. If we could go on. . .'

She could not let him continue. It was hopeless, and he was distressing himself. She would not look at him but kept her eyes down and said, 'I'm sorry, but you must know it's impossible.'

He had never been aware of her feelings as Tristram was. She had called him dull. But he understood now. He moved a little away and said, 'That young man with you . . .'

She did not answer, but suddenly it was all over. His voice changed to formal politeness – the voice she generally knew. 'I must apologise.' And he turned to the car.

She was not prepared for this sudden retreat. It was no good prolonging the encounter of course, but almost nothing had been said and she would have liked to soften her rejection. Outside Laurence's professional life, she realised, he was timid, though she did not know why. He had retreated after two sentences. She called after him, 'Anyhow – thank you.'

He paused but had nothing to say. She did not want him to go with a sense of grievance. She said, 'We shall meet again some time.'

'Of course. You're my patient.' And without saying good evening he got in and drove away.

But he was well disciplined. He rang up during the evening to say that Jos had telephoned and the Merediths had got home safely.

'Thanks,' she said, and would have liked to add some compliment. But there was nothing to say.

And then after the loss of the baby and the embarrassment with the doctor there came half a quarrel with Tristram. She quoted Shakespeare to herself about troubles coming 'in battalions'; then accused herself of exaggerating. All those busy people thronging the London streets must have similar arguments and disappointments.

At the time she was over busy, collecting paragraphs for her London Letter to tide over the five days she would have at home. The Christmas frenzy was on with an office party and piles of cards to be sent – to London people this year as well as to Birmingham and student friends. Laurence had already sent her an expensive flower card, and she must think of something, as impersonal as possible, for him.

And then the New Year was coming – the time when one reviewed one's life. In the past year she had settled into Fleet Street but beyond that seemed to have accomplished nothing. Months before Hughie had told her to talk to Tristram of her feelings, but she had not done so. They had drifted on. Her mother still thought she had some romantic link with Dr Gregg. That evening when she met Tristram the café had loops of tinsel and there was a surge of cheerful chatter. But she was oppressed by the thought that she would not see him for a fortnight, and in the New Year they would just go on meeting in the same way with the same coldness.

She began by asking him what he was doing for Christmas. He was not sure, he said. His aunts were free-thinkers and disliked the hypocrisy of the modern festival and shut themselves up with books. He had had several invitations. He might have a few days in Paris or go walking or perhaps just shut himself up like the aunts. She had said to him half seriously, 'Don't you get tired of never knowing what you're going to do?' and he said in his gently way, 'I suppose so', and that was the end of that.

The storm blew up when he asked her, for some unknown reason, what her friend the doctor was doing for Christmas. She always felt a stab at the heart when he mentioned Laurence, and she said she had no idea what doctors did at Christmas. Stayed on duty, she supposed. Old Jack would probably be with him, since the old man had nowhere to go.

Tristram said lightly, 'Why aren't you a better friend to the doctor?'

'Why should I be?'

'He seems to like your company.'

She was nettled at what seemed his indifference and said, asserting her own value, 'He does. He told me so the other day.'

'And you liked that.'

'*Tristram.*' There was a silence and then he said, 'Are you sure you won't be sorry later?'

He was offering her away as if there were nothing at all between them. She cried out, 'You don't understand anything, do you?' and he looked away and said nothing. But she could not bear dissension, and she said, 'Never mind. I've had a busy week,' and began to talk of her visits to the Christmas shows in shops. He listened with his gentle interest, but the shadow remained, and it was not long before he said, 'We'd better go.'

In the street she begged for the usual assignment. 'We'll meet on the usual day when I get back?' And he said, 'I suppose so. Happy Christmas,' but casually. He walked off and she watched and willed him to turn, but he did not.

When she got home she decided that this could not continue. Perhaps he really did not know her feelings. It was cowardly to write, but she could not speak out at their meetings. She put the pile of cards aside and wrote her letter many times but ended by sending only half-a-dozen lines. 'You behave as if you had no idea of my feelings. But you must know that I have loved you since we first met and I shall go on loving you. I think you should recognise this.'

The next day she had a Christmas card from him – an Alfred Sisley view of a winter avenue – without a message. She did not send a card back.

Two days after Christmas Anna and her mother called at The Hollies. Helena had written to Anna, 'You and Dr Gregg have changed our lives. We're in a frightful muddle and we don't yet know how we shall all settle down, but the world has become tremendously interesting.'

The music room at The Hollies seemed full of people. Benedict was away at a conference in America, but Rose had come down from Yorkshire and Jenny Owen was playing with the children. Mrs Dean joined in the adult talk, but Anna went across to Cindy's rug near the Christmas tree.

But the baby was no longer Cindy. She had become Kate and already she was a different child. Jenny and Irene were kneeling by the rug shaking a rattle and then putting it into her hand. The baby always dropped it, but you could not tell if she could not hold it or was letting it go on purpose. Each time she dropped it Jenny cried, 'Little naughty,' and the baby gave a half smile. She was already playing games.

She was not a pretty child with her thin red hair and wide mouth but she was strong, squirming about on her cushions. The other two kept setting her straight but she tumbled sideways again. Each time Jenny stooped to her the baby tried to get hold of her hair.

It was a contrast to the blank child in the cot, but the new Kate must have kept some recollection of the past. When she saw Anna she made the familiar little cry and waved her arms. Helena was going to and fro with tea. She was dishevelled in a long overall but she had pink cheeks and looked years younger. She called to Anna, 'Pick her up if you like,' and Anna stooped and took Kate, and the baby made the old movement of putting her hand to Anna's lips. But she was not as easy to hold as before, wriggling about and getting hold of a tuft of Anna's hair. Anna took her to the Christmas tree and she stretched at the lights and tore at a branch. 'She's very naughty,' Irene said with pride.

Anna walked her up and down with the other children poking the rattle at her. But then Helena came near and the baby lurched forward so that Anna could hardly hold her. She began to howl and Helena came quickly and took her. The child stopped howling and burrowed into Helena's shoulder, and Helena said, stroking the wispy red hair, 'Nowadays I can't call my life my own.'

In a way it was a bitter moment. Anna's arms were empty again and Cindy has gone. But in the bustle and laughter of that evening at The Hollies was born a new goal, a determination to face the future. Anna was seized with the wonder of growth. The screaming black-headed bundle in Laurence's surgery had become this stout child who already knew people and could play games. And if it happened this time it could happen again. Somewhere in the world would be another infant, and it would hold out its arms to Anna and burrow into her shoulder.

This would be her protection from Tristram. Anna would no longer be helpless before his indifference. She would have her own source of strength. Perhaps even she could draw him into this world of growing life. Her child could not come yet of course. She, Anna, was only twenty-three, but she would work and save and think of the future. She would no longer return to her flat agonising on some chance remark that he had made but would think, 'I must be strong-minded for the child's sake.'

She needed this new shield when she returned to London. Among the heaped letters inside her door was one of Tristram's thick white envelopes with his fine italic hand. But the letter inside was typed which made it more official and deadly.

It could hardly have been worse. He said that he was not worth her trouble. He had never asked for her love and was not a person to be loved. He was cursed with periods of despair when life became intolerable. At these times he was simply not fit to be alive. He did not talk about them to his friends, and he mentioned them now only because she was wasting her life with him. 'You have been a most sympathetic companion, but you have become too much involved. I have tried to show you, but you wouldn't see. Would it not be better if we ceased to meet?'

There was the vision of the baby ahead. It helped in the sickness of Anna's heart. It might even in the end do something for Tristram himself. She wrote back, 'Aren't you too much making a Byronic hero of yourself? Everybody feels melancholy at times, but there are cheerful things in life too. I don't want to be a nuisance, but I do want to go on seeing you. Give me what you can. I'll be there on Thursday.'

On Thursday he was outside the café as usual. They talked about Christmas which he had spent walking in Lincolnshire of all places. Neither of them mentioned the letters.

Jenny met Hughie Dean on a Saturday morning in March. He had come to the shop to buy an ice-cream before he went up to a local farmer to look at his van. Several times Jenny had seen Hughie about in his well-polished car as he visited friends of Edward Carey's to service their vehicles. He seemed to be doing well with his one-man business.

Hughie also seemed to have grown taller and was quite a man – eighteen at least. Jenny was feeding the hens and thinking she would have to spend the afternoon at homework as the Meredith family was going to Worcester. She had talked rather shyly with Hughie when he had worked on her father's van, and she was not sure how much she was supposed to know him. So she was surprised and gratified when he said, 'Like to come for a drive this afternoon?'

'Oh,' she said with one of those horrible blushes, 'are you going anywhere?'

'I've got to go up to Lane End to do a van and they've said they'll give me dinner. But I should be free after three.'

Jenny said falsely and deliberately, 'Well, I think I could make time,' and he whirred away. She felt a mixture of elation and timidity. She had been a bit worried about herself recently. The girls at school were always talking about boyfriends and dating, but she had nobody to talk about except Crabby, and she could hardly call him a boyfriend. She called him 'my country boy' to the girls and boasted that he had got a job in the big Hollies gardens through her. But Hughie Dean was somebody quite different – two years older and a gentleman.

During dinner, which she had with her mother and gran, Jenny casually mentioned that Hughie Dean had asked her to go for a ride. Mrs Owen, knowing Jenny, knew that it was no good making suggestions as to behaviour. So she only said, 'He's a good boy. Don't have any of your adventures.' Jenny replied that she did not have adventures, which was not quite true.

After dinner she went upstairs to make herself beautiful. The coast was clear as her mother was in the shop, her father was eating his dinner in the kitchen, and Gran had gone back to her cottage. Jenny put on her best blue blouse and, though it was a chilly day, her short red jacket. She had one pair of high-heeled shoes which were very uncomfortable but smart. After brushing her shoulder-length hair she adjusted her best diamond slide. Then she went to her mother's room to search for beautification.

She looked into a drawer and found some face-powder and perfume. It was a pity that Mrs Owen did not use lipstick and eye-shadow, but the Parfum d'Amour was pretty strong. It had been sent at Christmas by a fashionable second cousin in Smethwick. Jenny daubed herself; then surveyed herself from several angles in Mrs Owen's dressing-table mirror. She hoped that she looked eighteen. She would have liked to find a packet of cigarettes that she could offer to Hughie, but unfortunately her parents did not smoke.

She slipped out and stood in the road. At that moment Crabby came out of Gran's cottage. He had a room there now to allow another boy to be accommodated at Meadow Grange, but still went up there for his meals. He was working at The Hollies in the week, but this was Saturday afternoon. He stood a moment at the cottage door as if he did not know what to do, and then saw Jenny and came up for a talk.

Jenny, hoping she looked like a queen, said, 'Where are you going?'

'Well, I could go back to the home for TV,' he said gloomily, 'but I'm a bit sick of it with all those screaming kids.'

At that moment Hughie drew up in his car, and Jenny, partly out of kindness and partly because she was shy at being alone with Hughie, said, 'Can Crabby come too?'

Hughie seemed quite glad of the suggestion. He had chatted freely with Jenny while he was working at the Owens' van, but he too might be shy on this social occasion. He said to Crabby, 'All right. Hop in at the back.'

Then he began acting like a benign millionaire. He strapped Jenny in front and said, 'What about going to Bewdley and having a look at the river and getting some tea?'

This was to be a real outing. Jenny said, 'That would be *very* nice,' imitating the tones of one of her teachers, and they set off. There was silence for a moment and then Hughie said, 'There's a strong smell. Have you put something on your handkerchief?'

Jenny had Parfum d'Amour not only on her handkerchief but behind her ears. She had copied the girls in TV advertisements, not realising that, once it was there, you could not get rid of it in company. She said, not quite truthfully, 'My mother gave it me. It's a very expensive scent, but perhaps it's gone a little bad.'

There was silence again. It was a windy afternoon with the willows already yellow and some prunus trees making white clouds, but Jenny did not notice the scenery. She was racking her brains to think how she could make Hughie adore her.

Crabby was not much help. He was leaning back behind and humming 'The Ash Grove'.

Jenny had often wondered what lovers said to one another at corners. She thought they must be very personal things. The only personal thing she could think of to say to Hughie was, 'Have you any cats at home?'

'One.' He said no more. He was negotiating a busy traffic island.

When this was past she tried again. 'Did you have a nice dinner?'

'Steak and kidney pie. But it was a bit burnt.'

'Oh, what a pity. Do you like steak and kidney?'

'It's not bad.' Silence came down again.

Jenny continued to rack her brains and decided on something really daring. 'I suppose you know a lot of girls in Birmingham.'

'Only about two.' Another deadly silence.

Then Crabby stopped humming, and said, 'Mr Hughie, could you teach me to drive?' and Hughie at last seemed interested. A shouting interchange began between back and front about different makes of car. Jenny, feeling a little out of it, sat silent hoping she looked interested.

They came to Bewdley and crossed by the bridge, and Hughie said in his grand way, 'What about parking the car and having a cup of tea?' Jenny imitated her teacher again and drawled, 'That would be lovely,' but she began to feel more nervous. She would have to pour out the tea, and whenever she did it at home she spilt tea or the lid fell off. And should you put tea or milk in first?

Hughie was looking for a parking place when they came across a gang of boys in a narrow street. They were laughing and throwing paper and rubbish at a pigeon against a wall. The bird seemed unable to fly; would give a little jump and drop down again. One wing seemed useless.

As the car passed by a boy threw a carton and hit the bird. It fluttered and hopped along the wall, and another boy picked up a Coca-cola tin.

Jenny forgot that she was supposed to be a siren, and shouted to Hughie 'Stop.' The car went on a little and drew up, and she was quick in undoing her seat-belt and getting the car door open. She ran back, somewhat impeded by her high heels. Half-a-dozen big boys were picking up rubbish from the gutter to throw. One or two women with shopping bags had stopped to watch.

Jenny clicked up to the biggest boy and said, 'Stop it.' The boy looked down on her and said, 'Get out.' Another boy threw a carton and the pigeon fluttered and squawked.

Jenny was too angry to be frightened. Another boy laughed and said, 'Who do you think you are?' But one of the women sympathised with her. 'Them great lads ought to be ashamed of theirselves tormenting a poor creature.' More people stopped, and it looked as if a shouting match were developing. But Hughie and Crabby had got out of the car, and Hughie was taller than the boys. He said to the largest, 'Sheer off, will you,' in most impressive commanding tones. The boys hesitated.

'Crabby,' Jenny cried, 'get it.' She was the wistful princess no more but Boadicea. Crabby obediently went to pick up the pigeon, but a boy threw a stone which hit him on the leg. Then he too advanced on the boys doubling his fists. He looked, Jenny thought, like a thick-set English peasant standing up to the French at Agincourt. She had been 'doing' *Henry V* at school. But Hughie was the knight.

The boy who had hit Crabby backed, and Hughie, standing tall and bossy, said, 'If you don't sheer off I'll fetch the Police.' It was probably the first time in his life that he had commanded a crowd, but Jenny had been right. He had grown up.

He won. The boys slunk off, and the women went their ways. The street was nearly empty, and Crabby stalked the pigeon and caught it. 'Broken wing,' he said.

Jenny, instead of being a poor little unsuccessful girlfriend, was now in command. She said, 'Quick, let's get home. My dad knows a man who looks after birds.'

They tumbled back into the car, Crabby holding the bird firmly in spite of his maimed hand. He entertained them on the way back with tales of the terrible things that farm boys did to birds. They stopped outside the shop and Jenny ran in crying, 'Dad, we've got a poor pigeon.'

Mr Own called Jenny's mother to the counter and came out. He found a basket, took the pigeon and tramped off down the village to the man who helped him with the hens. The three stayed talking in the road till Mrs Owen handed back the shop and came out and offered them tea. She took a look at Jenny and said, 'What *have* you been doing with yourself?' but with the two boys present was too tactful to say any more.

She gave them tea in the small sitting-room and herself poured out the tea so that Jenny did not have to be nervous. Also Mrs Owen made easy conversation, asking Hughie about the farmers he had visited. Jenny, aware that she had been a heroine, very politely handed round cake.

The meeting had several results. The pigeon's wing healed, but the bird was still unable to fly far; so it joined the hens in the Owens' yard. Crabby had other meals with the Owens, and in the end had all his meals with Mrs Owen or Gran and did small jobs for the family as Alan had once done. And Jenny gave a dramatic account of the pigeon episode to her friends at school and ended by saying that she had decided never to marry but would be a vet. She might also get into parliament and make laws against boys' tormenting birds.

The Easter Benedict returned from Cambridge in the deepest depression. He was well into his PhD thesis on the Plinys and was preparing a book of selected translations with a short account of their lives. He seemed to have a university career ahead. He had even read a paper at a Californian meeting in December. He was unusual-looking, was always described as 'brilliant' and was a credit to the Carey family. Yet he was suffering bitterly. He had been betrayed by a perfidious woman.

In his first years at Cambridge he had been admired by several women students and learned that he could attract girls. He had shown off his knowledge, declared that he was a follower of Mithras and indulged in light flirtations. Then he had got tired of girls who, he said, had little minds. He turned to politics, hovered between Communism and the Labour Party, stewarded some meetings and then objected to the bad English of some of the speakers. He turned to Plato and declared that the rulers of a country should be the best educated, but then, looking at the mild feuds and prejudices among Cambridge dons, was not so sure. And then he met Olivia at a stall in the market-place.

She was quite old, at least thirty, and like Benedict world-weary. She had had some tragic love-affair that had ruined her life, and now she had a flat in Cambridge and coached students in the classics. At the market-stall Benedict began to talk to her about the Plinys and she made some sensible remarks. Soon they were meeting to discuss Latin writers.

With her horn-rimmed spectacles and brisk manner Olivia met him nearly every day. They made translations and compared them, and sometimes she gave him tea in her flat with harsh rye-vita and soft cheeses. She was witty and made fun of the lecturers they knew.

She had said that she would go with him to the Californian meeting, but at the last minute had to visit an aunt in Scotland. But she had returned to Cambridge for the spring term and had helped him by supplying background for the Plinys' lives. She was an experienced traveller and so was useful to Benedict who so far had not been beyond France. And then suddenly had come the bombshell.

Olivia had sent him a calm note saying that she was giving up her flat in Cambridge and was going to be married to some Edinburgh nonentity whom she had met in excavations of the Antonine Wall. She wished him well in his studies and would be glad to see him if he ever visited Edinburgh.

He came back to Ladyhill and told Helena, when she visited him for a talk in his room, that he would never trust anybody again. She began to tell him that the early twenties were a restless age and he would settle down later, but Kate, the new baby, woke up and began to scream in her pram, and Millie called Helena. That was another blow. In the old days Helena had had long discussions with him and he had instructed her on Latin writers of whom she knew little. He had liked instructing her. He considered that she had a good mind. But now she was always flying off because of the demands of the new baby, who seemed to rule the household. Everybody at Ladyhill seemed concerned with his own affairs, and here was he, Benedict, who in his childhood had been the chief care of the household, shut out.

On his second morning at home he went for a walk by himself. He had not yet seen Jenny, who usually haunted The Hollies when he was there. But now he saw her at a distance and at first was not sure if the slim dark-haired girl was Jenny. She seemed to have taken on a different figure in a few months. She had a slinky adolescent appearance and wore a red coat and red boots. He expected her to greet him with a soft appealing look but she only gave him a little nod and continued on the other side of the road.

So he said 'Hallo' and himself approached her. She was a nuisance, of course, but he had known her since she was born. However now, instead of lighting up with joy, she looked him up and down critically. He said rather patronisingly, 'How's school going?' thinking she would be gratified, but she stared up at the sky and said, 'Thank you. It's none of your business.'

This astonished him and at the same time made her seem more important. He said, in almost a conciliatory tone, 'You're always top of your class, aren't you?'

Jenny stopped looking at the sky and stared him up and down again. He was conscious that he was wearing old clothes and had not had a recent hair-cut. She said loftily, 'I don't want any more of your questions, thankyou, Mr Benedict. I've got more serious things to think about.'

Benedict was struck dumb. He stood a moment without even the courage to continue his walk. First Olivia had betrayed him. Now this simple village child, who generally bothered him with her admiration, was being beastly. He stood irresolute a moment; then went on and turned into the road to the pottery.

The place had changed, of course. The narrow track had been surfaced and the grass verges cut back. A long board with the name of 'Ladyhill Pottery' was now in front of the small brick building. Neat hyacinth-beds bordered the path, and the thicket had been partly cleared and a lawn made. But it had been Benedict's refuge in the old days, and he knew that Jos was inside.

Benedict opened the door and heard the wheel going at the back. The cottage room had changed too, with a table of Jos's bowls and vases and a side table with publications on arts and crafts. A desk held a new typewriter, and there was an electric fire. And Jos as he emerged was different – broader, with his hair less neatly trimmed. And yet, with his large spectacles, he was still Benedict's father figure, and he still kept his sarcastic tongue.

'You look as if you were off to a hanging.'

'I've just had a joust with Jenny,' Benedict said, shutting the door with a memory of old times.

'Did she fall on her knees and offer you primroses?'

'No, she hates me.'

'You'll be relieved.'

'I'm not. She was beastly.'

'Well I must say,' Jos said, 'you've asked for it.'

'Jos, I'm a kind of a pariah.'

'Dear me. I didn't know.'

'You needn't laugh. Alan goes through life expecting people to like him and they do. I expect people to hate me, and they always do.'

'And why is that?'

'I suppose because I'm inherently hateful.'

'Self-centred. Intolerant. Rude,' Jos said, but he was mocking.

'I suppose so.'

'All the same,' Jos said, suddenly serious, 'I owe you a debt.'

'*Me?*' Benedict did not believe at that moment that he had ever been of use to god or man. Yet now Jos looked at him kindly. 'You were the one who persuaded Helena to bother about me.'

'Did I?' It had been long ago when he was a schoolboy. He did not remember much of that argument with Helena, though it had changed all their lives. 'Oh yes . . . I went up to her when you said you were going to leave. I think I was frightfully rude.'

'You gave me what I most wanted. And now I see you going through life making things hard for yourself. Heaven knows I was a fool at your age, though I had the excuse of being a prisoner of war. You've got peace and a good brain, yet you come in here looking as if you were a lost spirit. But you know that if I can help you in any way I will.'

'It's nice of you Jos.' He was embarrassed. 'But you can't do anything. Nobody likes me.'

'Listen. One of your problems is that you're too remote. Can't you interest yourself in other people? Another is that you haven't enough to do down here. And with Helena so much occupied . . .'

'Do you like the orphan Kate?'

'She mustn't be called an orphan. And she's turning into such a tyrant that it doesn't matter whether I like her or not. It's whether she likes me. And she makes Helena happy.'

'And poor Irene doesn't get much attention.'

'It's all right. Kate makes Irene happy too. But what I want to say is this. Helena used to help me a bit with the business side of the pottery. Now she can't any more. Suppose you came here for an hour or two each day when you're home and dealt with the correspondence. You can type fairly well, can't you? You might be interested to visit some of the shows. And you might try your hand at potting if you liked.'

Did he really want somebody to help him or was he just being kind? Benedict did not know. But anyhow it was kindness, and it was extraordinary that Jos was grateful to him, and it would give him a chance to return regularly to the pottery that had been a refuge in his youth. He said, 'I'm glad you didn't go away Jos.'

'Really. I've sometimes thought you found me too much in evidence.'

'Life's so complicated.'

'Indeed. You don't mean it.' It was the old astringent Jos who had been one of Benedict's chief mentors in his boyhood. Now they reverted to the old habit of snacks and talks at the pottery. 'Let's have some coffee and I'll show you some of the hideous business letters.'

So they sat together, and Benedict said, 'To hell with Jenny.' And he thought he would make a figure of the Scarlet Woman and give her two heads, one of Olivia and one of Jenny.

On the first warm Saturday afternoon of the year Edward sat on a garden seat and meditated. He was still considering the enigma of memory, the memory that had continued in Mrs Noakes for more than twenty years and then compelled her to seize his hand. There were all sorts of questions to be asked. Many memories seemed to be hidden in the unconscious while one was aware of others. Why? Painful memories seemed less frequent than happy ones and even the painful ones came up softened. Was the best individual the one with the most happy memories?

Whatever the conclusion it came back to the old morality. Make as many people, including yourself, as happy as possible. Edward had plenty of opportunity to keep himself happy with the gardens and his family but precious little to do much for people outside Ladyhill. He thought of the owners of great organisations who every day met and influenced hundreds of people. Mrs Dean, with her factory welfare office, could help dozens. But here he was sitting alone on a garden seat.

As so often happens, the person whom he was considering appeared. The side gate opened and Mrs Dean came through. Her summer dress showed her as thin as ever, but as usual she was brisk and cheerful. On many Saturdays she came out to him while Dad was lost in television sport. She had telephoned that morning that she hoped to come, and Helena who had taken the call had said, 'Come and keep him company. We've got to go to Worcester to shop.'

Agnes Dean was a familiar visitor now, and there was no need of formal greetings. She came and sat beside Edward on the seat and said, 'What lovely scents. And there's Dad shutting himself up in our shabby sitting-room. He's on his own this afternoon. Hughie's off after another of his girls.'

Edward asked, 'How's Anna?'

'All right, I suppose. She talks less than she did. Hughie says she's involved with some writer, he thinks. Not Dr Gregg. She doesn't tell me.'

'We can't do much to influence them,' Edward said, thinking of his old days with Helena.

'Why should we want to?' In Mrs Dean's sharpness he sensed some worry about her daughter. 'Are we so clever ourselves?'

'You are. I'm not,' Edward said. 'I've been sitting here thinking of my uselessness. Come and get some tea. Millie's out.'

They went up to the big warm kitchen. Mrs Dean was an efficient companion, quick to find things, making tea without asking permission. Edward discovered some cake, and she took the tray down to the seat.

Continuing the conversation she said, 'You're forever talking of not being useful. Is it some form of pride?'

'Perhaps it's because I've got nothing else to worry about,' he said in his usual comic way.

The side gate opened again, and Jenny came through with Crabby behind her. The boy looked a little bashful. He had been there all the morning and had left without asking to come back. But Jenny was her confident self. 'Crabby's got nothing to do this afternoon. Would you like him to go on weeding? I could help him.'

'Hasn't your mother got jobs for you to do?'

'She's out with Gran. And Dad's in the shop. And I've done all my homework.' Then she burst out, 'Crabby thinks this an awfully dull village if you haven't got a car. I think so too.'

'All right,' Edward said. 'You can go and get some drinks from the kitchen. Go on with the vegetable beds but don't pull up the carrots and lettuces.'

The two went away and Mrs Dean asked, 'How's Crabby getting on?'

'He seems willing. And he's clever at using that injured hand of his. I shall do what I can for him. It's the first time I've heard that he's bored with the village.'

The two had come out and were now down the slope industriously bending over the vegetable plots with Jenny directing operations. Mrs Dean said thoughtfully, 'So he's got nowhere to go on Saturday afternoons.'

'He could go to Meadow Grange, but he seems to think the boys are too young for him.'

'And Jenny as well thinks that Ladyhill is dull.'

'I suppose it is for the young. They mostly go away.'

'Couldn't one somehow make it more interesting?'

'Perhaps. We've had competitions among the schoolchildren. Rose helped when she was here.'

'But still there's nowhere to go if you haven't got a car.'

'Ploughman's Arms. The vicar has meetings for his flock.'

'But teenagers. And what about the boys at Meadow Grange?'

'I've given them a bit of the field for their games.'

'And if it rains?'

'TV, I suppose. Yes, I know they're crowded. That's another thing that has worried me since I went to see Mrs Noakes. All those people jammed together and having no chance of being alone.'

'Well then, if you want to be useful. Some small leisure building . . .'

He said, 'It would cost a mint of money.'

'Could you get anybody else to help?'

'I don't know. You're like a gad-fly.'

'You bring it on yourself,' Mrs Dean said.

'Would you advise?'

'I'm not much good on buildings. Dad might have suggestions.' She added, 'Get Jenny and Co to help. She likes to be important.'

A moment later the two came up the slope. 'We're boiling. Can we have some more orange?'

Edward said, 'We're thinking of building a place where you can go on Saturday afternoons.'

Jenny threw up her fork and cried, 'Goody. Goody. Can I be chairman?'

Jenny began to write to the doctor that spring. Alan had brought him to stay again in February and, though it was cold, they had gone to Stratford and Jenny had been able to show him three valentines that had been sent her. The doctor had gone with Jenny to The Hollies to look at the new baby, and he had had a long and boring talk with Helena about adoption. Jenny had felt out of it as she knew little of the subject except that Snow White had been adopted by the dwarfs. So she played quietly with the children, and the doctor had said that she was a good nursemaid.

Then one of Millie's cats got a bad ear, and Jenny took the opportunity to write to the doctor for advice. Edward called a vet in so that advice was not needed, but it started off the correspondence with London. Jenny was proud of her neat handwriting, and the only trouble was that she did not know how to end her letters and was too proud to ask. So she wrote 'Yours faithfully', hoping that it would make the doctor realise that she would never forget him.

He sent her back very interesting letters about London and sometimes picture postcards. Once or twice he drew pictures of trains at Waterloo or Westminster Abbey. They were small drawings and not much better than Irene's but Jenny put them all, including the envelopes, away in her drawer. He signed his letters 'with love' which was beautiful, but Jenny still preferred 'Yours faithfully'.

She had plenty to write about that summer. There was Edward's idea of building a centre for leisure – and Jenny could spell it. Then there was the baby who was becoming a little devil. Or rather a big devil, for she was very large for her age and walked and climbed early. Kate liked fighting and had no sense of danger, and Jenny knew because in the school holidays Helena gave her two pounds a week to be with the children in the morning.

Kate never stopped getting into trouble, especially if they were in the garden. She climbed the rockery and could not get down, spiked her coat on a rose-bush so that she was suspended, and ate a bumblebee. Jenny wanted to know what the doctor thought about smacking. He replied that the baby seemed a bit young for punishment and Jenny had better speak to Helena. But Jenny did not speak to her. She knew what the answer would be.

The doctor came again with Alan in August, and there was talk of Alan joining him when he qualified. Jenny was a little jealous, but they had a lovely conversation on the doorstep where she had once sat with Rose. She had asked the doctor to speak to Crabby who had lately startled her by declaring that he was going to be a murderer.

He had seemed a quiet enough lad with his thatch of hair and pale eye-lashes but he had confided that when he was grown-up with a good job he would return to the farm where he had been brought up and would kill the farmer and his wife, and, if possible, the woman who was supposed to be his mother. These plans might partly be influenced by television, but Jenny was not sure. She said to the doctor while Alan was talking to his parents, 'Can I fetch my country boy to speak to you?'

Crabby had been at Gran's for lunch, and Jenny led him, rather untidy and sheepish, to the doctor, and they sat on the doorstep. The doctor was in the middle. He said, 'What's wrong?' And Crabby, in his slow slovenly speech, disclosed details of his youth. He had lived with the woman Win in a cottage of two rooms and the farmer had come at night and made silly noises. Crabby had not been allowed to play with the farmer's children and when the farmer's wife came across him she called him names. He had been watching the men scything grass by the road when his hand had got in the way and he had lost his fingers and had to go to hospital. When he returned to the farm it had been some of the men, not Win, who chiefly looked after him. There was a lot of shouting at the farmhouse and the farmer stopped coming to the cottage and Win took up with a new farm hand and one night the two disappeared. The farmer wrote to the Council and said he was not responsible for Crabby, and so the boy had been put into a home and finally had reached Ladyhill. Now he was going back to kill the farmer and his wife and some other people though not the men who had been kind to him.

He was quite open about this. He had seen lots of murders on television, and this was the usual way to behave. The doctor heard him through, and then quietly asked, 'Have you got a gun?'

No. Crabby had got no gun. But people on TV often used knives. Or he might get hold of some explosives. Jenny piped up then, acting the moral little girl, 'But it's wicked to kill people, isn't it doctor?'

For once he ignored her and said to Crabby, 'Are you prepared to go to prison for twenty years?'

Crabby said, 'I'd hide.'

'You'd be prepared to hide for the rest of your life?'

Crabby was not sure about that. Didn't the Police drop cases in the end?

'Not murder cases I'm afraid.'

After twenty minutes on the doorstep Crabby seemed a bit uncertain. He said, 'Well, I might not do it yet,' and the doctor made a remark that Jenny was to think over afterwards. 'If you're angry with anyone it's best to keep away.' Then he tried to cheer Crabby up by saying that if he worked hard Mr Carey would look after him. He had been talking to Frank Owen, Jenny's father, who had said that Crabby was lucky to be taken on at The Hollies.

Then Alan came, and the meeting broke up. Crabby told Jenny afterwards that it might be awkward to have to hide so much, and he really wanted to become a head gardener and keep bees. It had been nice to talk to someone who knew so much about policemen.

Meanwhile Jenny thought over the doctor's words about keeping away. She remembered that he had said that, except for a visit to Mrs Dean in Birmingham, he had not been to the Midlands for years. Jenny made up a lovely story, which she afterwards told to Irene, of how the doctor had had a wicked stepmother who had tried to murder him, and how he had jumped from a window while bullets whizzed around him. Then he had climbed a wall and walked to London. She thought of adding a faithful cat, but that was too much like something else. The doctor had arrived in London as a poor boy but by dint of hard work had become famous. He never went back to the Midlands until some kind friends invited him. The thought of his sufferings gave Jenny warm heart-beats as she lay in bed at night.

There was one more rather chaotic meeting before the doctor left. He and Jenny walked up to The Hollies to see the baby. Kate was sitting with Irene on the grass while Helena hung out some washing. She called, 'Half a sec'; so Jenny picked up the baby, who had been banging with an iron spoon on a tin. She was a mucky little thing with a dirty mouth from eating something unspeakable. She gave Jenny a whack on the head with the spoon, and Jenny, who practised acting to make her sorry, put her down and covered her own face with her handkerchief. Jenny hoped that the doctor as well as the baby would be sorry for her.

Unfortunately the doctor was talking to Irene who was showing him her drawing book with little bright-coloured numbers in corners and drawings of Rupert Bear, Millie's cats and the baby in the middle. When Jenny pretended to be hurt Irene, who must have been doing history at school, said 'Kate thinks she Poleon,' and the baby set up a tremendous howl. Helena came rushing and picked up the dirty baby and said, oddly, 'Isn't she a wonder?' and the doctor, who seemed equally blind, said, 'You've done a good job.' While they talked Jenny sat quietly with Irene, but the baby came behind and gave her another tremendous wop on the head with the spoon.

Jenny could not put her handkerchief over her face again. So she sat uncomplaining, and the doctor noticed and said, 'You're very patient with her,' which was not quite accurate as Jenny was often furious. Then Helena made up for some of her past awfulness by saying, 'Jenny's our chief nursemaid.'

Somewhere in the house on that happy afternoon was Benedict, who now did not matter more than a fly. All the same Jenny hoped that he was looking out of a window.

They did not stay long as the doctor and Alan had to get back to London. But the doctor would come again, and meanwhile there would be those splendid letters. Jenny always sniffed them to see if the smelt of some divine disinfectant, but generally they smelt only of paper. But the postmark, if you could read it, was impressive, showing that they really did come from London.

Jenny said, as they approached the stores with the doctor's car already outside, 'Why did you come back to the Midlands, doctor?'

'I suppose because the Owens invited me.'

'Do you like the Owens?'

'Very much.'
'*All* the Owens?'
'Particularly the girl, of course.'

Jenny looked up at him and thought again that he was like one of those Wild West heroes with his strong face; only his hair was short. She would never forget that compliment, but for once words failed her.

Anna and Tristram had spent a tranquil summer. She had made few demands, and they had talked of literature and art, and he had lent her books. She had been with her family to the Broads because Hughie was growing interested in motor-boats, and on one or two evenings, watching sunset over the expanses of still water, she had wondered what Tristram would have done with it. Then she had returned to London and they had met in the usual way. The meetings were part of her life, and she had little fear now of their ending.

He had been taking one or two classes and sorting his father's papers. He no longer brought her his writing to criticise, and this hurt her a little. But she would not be hurt, and she would not harass him with enquiries. She protected herself by thinking of her child, the future child, not yet begotten, not yet from any place, but at some future time to burrow its head into her shoulder as Kate burrowed into Helena's.

She told no-one about it. The men at the office who had seen her with Tristram made jokes about 'Little Miss Dean's sweetheart'. She laughed too to keep them off and said she would invite them to the wedding. She noticed that her mother at home had stopped talking of 'Anna's doctor', but Mrs Dean made no direct enquiries. Hughie, who seemed to have a different girl every time that Anna went home, exhorted her once or twice to cheer up. She kept him off too. She was afraid of mentioning that future child, as she suspected that there might be some protest.

Old Jack still came to her flat, did jobs for her and talked. He told her when Laurence visited Ladyhill, and she wondered idly how they had liked him there. Since that abortive approach outside her flat he had half dropped out of her life, except that Jack talked about him so much. She had thought of visiting Mrs Noakes's old friends at the Garden Home, but did not because she did not want to meet

Laurence. Yet, when she thought of it, she was sorry for his loneliness in a way she was never sorry for Tristram.

And then, without warning, the tranquil world collapsed. It was in November, and Anna had a cough. Tristram too seemed to have a cold and looked pale, but she did not comment. She tried to avoid any personal questions.

They were easy at first, used to one another, drifting into talk without having to explain who the people they mentioned were. She had been home for the week-end and described how she and her mother had gone out to Ladyhill and how Kate, the baby, now over a year old, was turning into a gymnast. 'She runs about like a two-year-old, but she's a bit slow in talking. Her chief word seems to be "won't".'

Was he interested in children? He said he knew little about them. From his own memories of childhood he thought they had experiences which they lost as they grew up, but they never told the parents who looked after them, and the parents with their training and rules seemed to be trying all the time to turn children into little adults. Anna remembered the first writing of his that she had seen about the girl in the rose-garden who did not want to grow up. She said now, 'Men and women seem to differ in their attitudes. Men, like you, remember their own childhoods and feel that their personalities were damaged. But women look at the children round them and know that they have to be trained.'

He said lightly, 'Are you going to train children, Anna?'

She had told him many things about her life but not that one thing. But she had always imagined that he would be there when she found her shadowy child, and there seemed no need to keep the idea from him. She said, 'Yes, I am.'

'How?'

'I'm going to adopt a child later on as Helena adopted Kate.'

He was suddenly hostile. 'What nonsense!'

She looked at him surprised. '*You*? Being conventional.'

He said, 'I don't know whether I'm being conventional or not, but it would be idiotic for you.'

'Why should it be? We're not living in Victorian times.'

'You're too young to make such decisions.'

'Oh, I shan't do it for years. But I'm beginning to save up.'

'I think it's utterly wrong,' he said more harshly than she had ever heard, and this roused her own temper and she said, 'I must have some warmth in life; some human contact. We sit week after week discussing Shakespeare and Racine, and then I go home and I feel so frustrated, so humiliated.' She realised as she spoke that she was baring feelings that she had hardly been aware of before. But it was true.

He said, 'I thought you wanted these meetings.'

'I do, of course. But – no you won't see.'

She felt as if she were on the edge of an abyss and stopped. He said, still urgently, 'What about taking the conventional way?'

'Marriage? How can I? How can I?'

'You mean I'm stopping you.'

'Yes. No. There's nobody else. You know how I feel.' Long afterwards she was glad that she had made that confession.

He sat thinking and then said, 'This can't go on.'

'You don't mean you won't see me,' she said in a panic.

'I don't know. I must think. We'd better go.'

She said again, 'But we must go on meeting.'

She had at that moment a feeling that he was very kind. He stood up and said, 'I didn't mean to cause all this havoc. I'm sorry. I'll write.'

He paused a moment by the door. 'It's been a good experience.'

It sounded like some farewell. She was frightened and said, 'You won't go away?'

'I'll let you know. Of course I want you to be happy.' For a moment they stood in the doorway, and then he said 'Goodnight.' He did not wait for her but walked away and disappeared among the people in the crowded wet street.

It was only the next evening that the bell pealed at Anna's door. The time had seemed much longer, and all day she had been going over their last argument.

She was tired and with a sore throat. She had got home at seven, but half an hour later, when the bell rang, she was still sitting idle by her fire. She thought it was Jack who had forgotten his key and went down unwillingly, but at the door stood a small grey-haired woman with an intelligent face and a long unfashionable blue coat. Anna thought vaguely, 'I have seen those brown eyes before.'

The old woman looked at her with an enquiring gaze and said 'Anna?' It did not seem strange that she should know Anna's name.

Anna With Tristram

It was like a dream in which people are suddenly there and know you.

Anna said, 'Yes. I'm Anna Dean,' and waited.

The old woman said, 'May I come in for a minute, my dear?'

Anna led the way upstairs. The light in her sitting-room glared. The old woman was wet, but she did not take off her coat. She said, 'Sit down, my dear.'

Anna knew absolutely what the old woman was going to say. The light began to waver.

'I am afraid you will be shocked. We found my nephew this morning – lying downstairs . . .'

'You mean?'

'Yes.'

Anna thought, 'I should be feeling something,' but she felt nothing. She looked at the old face and thought, 'There is a family likeness.' She asked, 'But how . . . ?'

'We don't know yet. We may want your help. You were with him yesterday, weren't you?'

The room seemed very cold. 'Yes.'

'Did anything happen to upset him?'

'You don't mean . . . ?'

'We're not sure, my dear. There will be an inquest.'

'He couldn't surely have done that.' She could not stop shivering.

'He'd had a troubled life. We shall know later. We just wondered if you could help us.'

The visitor spoke steadily. She was a spartan old woman.

Anna said, 'We had tea. He didn't seem very well. We had an argument . . .'

'But nothing that would explain it?'

'I don't know. I don't know.' So she had done it. She had known that he had these fits of melancholy and yet she had harried him with her complaints. He had gone away desperate; gone home . . . She would never get over it. She was damned for ever. She could answer no more questions now. She said, 'Can I ring you later?'

The old woman said, 'I've given you a shock. I'm sorry,' gently as Tristram might have said it. 'If you would telephone me later. I must get back to my sister now. I can let myself out.' She turned at the door in an effort at comfort. 'You were a good friend to him.' And Anna thought, 'Friend! And I've killed him.'

The old woman went down the stairs. She had been there for less than a quarter of an hour. After a time the bell went again. Anna did not answer at first, but it went on pealing. At last she got up languidly, and this time it was indeed old Jack. He said, 'I've brought you that bulb you wanted, but I've forgotten my key.'

Anna said, 'Please, not tonight.'

He glanced at her; then looked again. 'What's up miss?'

She did not answer, and he said, 'I'd better fetch the doctor.'

She cried, 'No. You're not to,' but he had gone.

After some minutes the bell went yet again. Again she did not answer at first and again it went on ringing. In the end she went down again and opened the door a crack. It was Laurence, of course. She said, 'Please go away.'

But he did not listen. He pushed the door open and came in. He asked, 'Is it Tristram?'

In a strange way there was comfort in hearing the name. She went back to her sitting-room and the doctor followed. She said loudly, 'Tristram's dead.'

She saw his startled look and had some pleasure in passing on bad news. 'And I've killed him.'

But Laurence said, 'He can't be. He was talking to me yesterday evening.'

'*You?*'

'He called at my surgery.'

'But he didn't know you.' In all her shock she was still angry that Tristram had spent some of his last hours with a stranger instead of with her.

He tried to soothe her. 'People in trouble often come to doctors.'

'And then go home and kill themselves.'

'What?'

'If he did come to you as you say you didn't do him much good. He went away and . . .'

The doctor asked, 'Who said it was suicide?'

'His aunt. She found him.'

He thought for a moment, searching his memory. 'It wasn't. It couldn't have been suicide.'

For a moment something eased inside her. Was he rescuing her from this torture of guilt? But she did not believe him. She said, 'How do you know?'

'Listen. He came because he wanted advice.'

She said, 'And you said something to make his despair.'

'He was not in despair.'

In her misery she did not care what she said. 'You're not telling the truth. I'd hurt him and you made him worse.'

Jack had come back. He said from the stairs, 'You didn't ought to talk to the doctor like that.'

But Anna took no notice. She said to Laurence, 'Please don't come here again.'

Then the room began to turn and she was lying back with perspiration on her forehead. She heard him repeating, 'It was not suicide. It was not suicide', and there was some slight relief if she were not guilty after all. She should have been grateful for release from the nightmare, but she was past feeling anything. She heard the doctor say to Jack, 'Go and fetch Marion.' Marion was the surgery nurse. Then from somewhere Laurence said, 'She can't be left alone.' Then she shut her eyes struggling with faintness.

Later the nurse was there and Jack had gone. The nurse helped her to undress and got her into bed. All Anna wanted was to lie down. The nurse gave her some pills and she went to sleep.

In the morning Marion brought her a cup of tea and a letter. Anna had the sense to ask Marion to telephone her office and say that she was not well. Then Marion took her temperature and said she had better stay in bed for the present. The world seemed a long way away, but Anna had the letter in her hand.

She recognised it of course – the thick white envelope and fine italic hand. For a moment she thought that Tristram might not be dead after all, but then she looked at the postmark and it was of two days previously. He must have gone straight out after seeing the doctor and caught the late post.

For several minutes she had not the courage to open it. Then she opened it very carefully. It was already a relic. There would not be any more. There was half a page in his own writing inside. It began, 'My dear Anna' and it was affectionate without the usual reserve. He said that she had been one of the best friends he had ever known, and their meetings had meant a great deal to him. He would have been glad to go on, but he was aware that he was disappointing her all the time. 'I have told you that I am not fit to be loved.' Now that she had brought her dissatisfaction into the open he had considered the situation again and had gone to Dr Gregg for advice. The doctor had advised him to continue for a time in the hope that they would work something out. 'He wanted, I think, to spare you pain.' But on reflection, Tristram had disagreed. If they continued he would only go on causing her unhappiness. So he had decided to return to Paris for the present. 'Perhaps later when we are older and free-er we can meet again.'

So Laurence had been right. Whatever had happened it had not been suicide. She did not have to suffer the frightful pain of guilt. And Tristram had looked forward to a time when they might meet again.

But he had gone. She lay back comforted by the letter but facing the appalling chasm of emptiness. She thought she must apologise to Laurence, but then the room began to swim again and she had a pain in her chest. The nurse propped her up, and she was aware of voices below and Laurence was there. She had not strength to apologise, but she took more pills and went to sleep again.

When she woke the nurse had gone, and someone else was in the room.

The figure came and stood by her bed. It was her mother.

In those dark winter weeks when Anna was in bed with bronchitis the telephone rang continually. She had more London friends that she had realised, but they seemed a long way away, a crowd of kind chattering people who did not matter. Her mother answered the telephone and seemed to say the same thing each time. 'She'll be all right later on.'

But 'later on' had not yet arrived. She was confused. The doctor came in once or twice at the beginning, but Anna left her mother to talk to him. She suspected that Mrs Dean also went across to the surgery where they could talk freely. Mrs Dean kept the flat tidy and cooked and went out for short periods to shop. Jack came in, talked to her of his war experiences and ran errands.

The nights were worst. Anna dropped off to sleep in the day, but at eleven at night she was hot and her eyes would not close. She got up one night and stood looking over slate roofs glinting in the street lights and cars flashing in the distance; and she wondered if there was any decent way of getting out of life.

Her mother found her by the window and must have gone to the doctor, for the next evening Anna had stronger pills and slept. For a day or two she lived in a maze of half-sleep. And then something happened that opened up a gleam of light.

Her mother came from the telephone and said, 'It's Tristram's aunt.' Anna was surprised that Mrs Dean knew the name. It must be from the doctor. It was a relief to hear it spoken after all that silence, and Mrs Dean said, 'She wants to come and see you again. There's been an inquest, and it was natural causes – heart. It's in the family.'

Anna said, 'Thank her. I should like to see her.' She wanted to look at the old face again and see the Tristram image.

The next afternoon Mrs Dean opened the door to the figure in the long blue coat. Mrs Dean said, 'If you don't mind I'll take the opportunity to get a little shopping done. I shall be back in about half an hour.' It was her way of giving Anna a chance of free conversation.

Miss Forrest sat by the bed, and Anna watched her. The old woman understood as Tristram might have done, and said, 'He was more like his mother, but he had our eyes.'

She seemed brisk and calm. She was a strong-minded woman. She said, 'I've come with a request. You know about literary matters, He has left a desk-ful of papers.'

'What do you want me to do?' Anna thought. 'Thank God. It would be a way of getting some contact.'

'My sister and I are old and our eyesight isn't too good. And we've been teachers. We don't know about literary matters. But you do.'

'Only journalism.'

'You know the market. Didn't you meet Tristram through that?'

'I've got to go home,' Anna said. 'My mother doesn't want me to be up here alone.' The offer was such an overwhelming relief that she could afford to accept it slowly.

'But you'll be back, won't you?' Miss Forrest said.

'I expect so. My office has given me leave until after Christmas.' And she thought, 'This is one thing that will make my return bearable.'

'Then come and see us then.' The old lady looked at Anna's flushed face and, as she got up, offered what comfort she could. 'He was not unhappy all the time. He could be very amusing and he had many friends. But you were the one he saw most often, and it did him good to talk.'

Anna got better slowly after that. A fortnight went by and Mrs Dean began to talk of a return home. 'Poor Dad will have been having the most horrible time. He's living on bread and cheese.' Hughie would come and fetch them in his car so that the journey would be easy.

Anna had only one more long conversation before they left. Laurence came in to check that she was fit to travel, and, as before, Mrs Dean left them alone, and went into the little room to pack.

Anna apologised before he made the usual checks. 'I was mad the other day. I don't know what I said.'

If he had been angry he did not show it. 'People say all sorts of things when they are ill. You can forget it.' She had the impression that he was being very careful to keep her calm.

He said at the end of the examination, 'You can go home, but you'll have to be careful for the rest of the winter.'

Foolishly she angled for his pity. 'Does it matter?'

But he did not soften. 'Indulgence in self-pity won't help you.' She had the feeling that perhaps he had said the same thing to himself.

But he was a link with Tristram – the last person to have seen him alive. She still did not understand why Tristram had been to him, and she appealed while the doctor shut his case. 'Was Tristram worried about his health?'

'I offered to examine him, but he refused.'

'The heart attack – it couldn't have happened because he had been with me?'

'Unlikely. He seemed quite calm. It can happen at any time.'

She changed the drift of her questions. 'I told him I was going to adopt a child. He utterly disapproved.'

'I know. He mentioned it.'

'Why did he disapprove? He wasn't conventional.'

Laurence was slow to answer. 'Perhaps he didn't think it was the right solution for you.'

'Yet he was leaving me.'

He turned to go and spoke quite harshly. 'Doctors can't pass on things that patients say in confidence. I really can't tell you any more.'

He sounded annoyed but he relented to say, 'Get better soon' as he went to say goodbye to Mrs Dean.

Jenny became an angel that Christmas.

She sent thirty-four Christmas cards, and began the holidays in a glow of righteousness because she had done well at school. She was determined to help everybody, including, of course, the hens. She had been kind before, but now she was important as well.

She was the secretary of a committee – the committee on Uncle Edward's leisure centre. People came and went on the fortnightly committee, but Jenny never missed a meeting. She sat at the end of the long table in the music room, and opened operations by reading the minutes. She had two books, one for making notes and the other for writing them out nicely. Uncle Edward signed the neat version, and she kept the books in her handkerchief drawer at home. Uncle Edward said that the neat book would be kept as a treasure in the centre when it was finished.

Uncle Edward generally had something good to report. The centre was being built at the top of the field next to Meadow Grange. The boys were extending the Meadow Grange garden to go round it, and there was to be a passage between the two buildings so that the boys could run through in wet weather. But the door was to be locked so that other people could go there when the boys did not want it.

Jos had an architect friend in London who did the design, and Ken Burrows, the local builder, and another local man were doing the work. It was to be a wide brick building of two storeys, and Uncle Edward was having two seats placed behind it so that anybody who wanted to be quiet could sit outside and look down the green slope.

Uncle Edward did most of the business, and four firms were contributing quite large sums of money. But there were questions to be discussed in committee, and Jenny raised her voice. It had been decided from the first that the centre should be for the whole village, but how much were the Ladyhill people to contribute to the furnishings? Some of them were having television sets and fridges installed and so had bits of furniture they did not want. Edward said he was willing to pay for the furnishings, but Jenny piped up and said very sensibly, she thought, that if people gave things they would be more interested. Ken Burrows said that gifts that were not needed could go into a jumble sale to make more money, and so appeal notices were poked through village doors. Jenny helped to distribute them.

She was happy with her committee work and had told her school friends about it. But there were other good things that winter. The wicked Kate was beginning to improve. This was surprising because her mother, Helena, thought she was the Queen of Sheba, and Irene was such a peaceable little thing that she would have made a saint selfish. But Jenny was trying to discipline Kate to behave like a decent human being. She did it mainly by a rewards system of the kind you use with animals. If Kate did not kick anybody for a whole morning or if she did not scream or jump on Irene she got a chocolate or a peppermint (mild). Jenny brought these up in a bag as a gift to the household. Helena did not know about the sweets that Kate consumed, but actually there were not an awful number because Kate's behaviour was not yet perfect.

But Kate liked turning somersaults and being held by the ankles up-side-down, and Jenny gave her these exercises. This made Kate sleep better in the afternoon. Jenny was also trying her with nursery rhymes, and she liked the more violent ones such as 'Chip chop, chip chop, last man's dead' and 'Jack fell down and broke his crown'. Helena, when she read to the children, tried to keep away from death and fighting, but Kate enjoyed both.

As a result of Jenny's efforts Kate sometimes gave her a wet kiss. She also liked to pull Jenny's shoulder-length hair saying 'Ding, dong bell.' Jenny took this as a mark of affection.

Other people liked Jenny of course. Hughie Dean had asked her and Crabby to another car ride. They went to see a motor-cycle scramble and it was very boring, but Hughie and Crabby seemed to enjoy it. Afterwards they had a pot of tea and crisps at a café and Jenny poured out without spilling the tea. She often saw Hughie because he had a regular business now of servicing cars, and he seemed happy, having passed some exams.

Crabby she saw every day. He had moved into Alan's room at home, except when Alan cam down from London and then Crabby went back to Gran's. He was learning to take cuttings and sow seeds and later Edward might send him to some course at Pershore. He said that he had decided not to go back to the farm of his youth. It was enough punishment for the farmer to have that awful wife. And now he was going to have Christmas dinner with the Owens.

Jenny did other angelic deeds. She helped in the shop and was very quick with the arithmetic. She did not like housework, but cleaned her own room without complaint. She did not read her Bible as Gran had told her, but she collected her old toys and took them to the vicarage for a Christmas distribution among the poor children of the housing estate.

Her most delicious job was to find a card for Dr Gregg. Her mother took her in to Worcester and she spent nearly half an hour going through cards at a stationer's. She wanted something to make the doctor happy, but many of the comic cards seemed vulgar. In the end she chose a big card of a cat at a window because the doctor had not got one. She wrote inside 'My best wishes' and then her usual, 'yours faithfully, Jenny'. Already some parcel with a card had come from him. She had not opened the parcel but had looked at the card and had kept it in her bosom.

One old feud came to an end in quite an easy way. Benedict Carey was home for Christmas and was still talking about his beastly Plinys but also helping Jos at the pottery. Jenny met him in the road, and he was going by without noticing her, but it was a season of good will and she was feeling mischievous. So she crossed over and said, 'How are you doing at college, my little man?' He stared at her for a moment and then burst out laughing and said, 'You're the limit.' 'You are too,' Jenny said, and so their peace was made. Benedict attended one of the committee meetings and said afterwards that she ought to be chairman of the Royal Society. She did not know what the Royal Society was or if it had a chairman, but she took it as a compliment.

At the last committee meeting of the year just before Christmas Mrs Dean and Anna came out. They had returned from London the week before, and Jenny was a bit shocked when she saw Anna. Jenny had always admired this girl who looked so young but was said to be a famous journalist. But now she was frightfully pale and was given an armchair by the fire while the committee met round the table. Kate seemed fond of Anna and kept climbing on to her knee, but Anna did not seem to have much energy to play; just lay back and let the baby pat her face.

At the end of the meeting Jenny, being an angel, went to cheer Anna up. She knew that Anna lived near the doctor, and she said, 'Shall I show you something?'

'If you like,' Anna said in a limp way; so Jenny fished in her bosom and brought out an envelope. Inside was a home-made card. '*He* sent it,' Jenny said.

It was not a very well drawn picture of two people, presumably the doctor and old Jack, sitting at a table marked 'Christmas Cheer' and chewing two large bones. Above on a looping string was a row of tiny squares meant to be letters and on each in tiny capitals was 'From Jenny'.

'We write a lot to one another,' Jenny said.

The card made Anna laugh. 'I shouldn't have thought he had it in him,' she said.

'He's a kind of Charlie Chaplin,' Jenny asserted, 'But Charlie Chaplin wasn't a doctor.' After that Anna looked pinker.

Tristram's aunts sat in their warm neat sitting-room and talked of their lives. They were alike and yet different. Beatrice, the older sister, was taller, thinner and quieter. Margaret, who had visited Anna, talked more and was more active. Beatrice had arthritis and looked after the house. Margaret did the shopping and gardening.

Both had taught English abroad. Beatrice in France and Margaret in Denmark. At the outbreak of war they had to return with their lives in ruins, but they had taken small teaching and lecturing jobs till retirement age. After so many years abroad they had hardly known one another but they had decided to live together and the ménage had worked. They had moved to Hampstead after the war to be near their brother's family. Now they did not complain and paid one another compliments, but Beatrice said, 'We know very few young people,' and Anna suspected desolation there.

She had arrived in mid-afternoon and had been given tea. She had enjoyed their stories but after an hour had begun to wonder if they had changed their minds about the papers. All through her convalescence she had had the hope of somehow getting into touch with Tristram again. She had come out to Hampstead as to a shrine, but had been met with anecdotes of Denmark and France.

But they were straight old women. They would not have deceived her. She learnt afterwards that it was difficult for them to mention Tristram's name, and Margaret had seen Anna in her illness and was afraid of upsetting her again. But they did not flinch in the end. After tea Margaret said, 'If you're not too tired – the papers are down the road.'

She and Anna put on coats and went out into the windy darkness. Anna's heart was throbbing. This was the centre of her earth. But then it was no holy shrine; only a small brick house a few doors from the aunts', with a gate that stuck and the tall blowing heads of weeds and a neglected lawn. Margaret apologised. 'Our brother was a gardener, but Tristram was not. He was too much of a wanderer. And I haven't been able to do much in the last few months.'

She opened the front door and there was more desolation – rolled-up carpets and disordered furniture against walls. She said, 'We are having to sell most of the stuff. We haven't room.' But then came the sight that Anna had never hoped to see. Margaret opened a bedroom door and switched on a light. She said, 'We've left his room in case you wanted to sit here.' And there was the Tristram shrine.

Anna was aware of the melancholy figure of Watteau's 'Gilles' on a wall, with some pen and ink sketches of café figures, probably from

Anna With Tristram

friends. A large photograph of Snowdon hung in a corner. That must have been his mother's. There was a bookcase stretching almost to the ceiling, and a large old-fashioned desk scattered with papers. A small bed at the back had not apparently been touched.

Margaret pulled the long green curtains, switched on an electric fire and said, 'We thought you might like to be left alone to look through the papers. I'll be back at 6.30.' It was a gesture of kindness. She went down the stairs and there was silence.

Anna would have liked to try an experiment. The spirits of the departed are supposed to linger round the places they have known. She would have liked to sit still and wait. But there was the large desk, and Margaret was coming back in an hour.

She began to open drawers and put papers into piles. But it was soon evident that sorting would take weeks. Tristram had written far more than he had ever shown her or mentioned – verse, travel sketches, the beginnings of two novels, translations. The first task was to separate out the bills, catalogues and art notices. She had hardly done that when Margaret returned.

Sitting surrounded by piles of papers, Anna cried, 'I've done nothing. There's too much.'

'You mean you don't want to sort them?'

'I do. Of course I do. But then what?' An idea came to her like a command. 'They ought to be made into a book.'

'Is there enough?' Margaret said doubtfully. It was clear that Tristram had kept his work from his aunts too.

'Enough? Look. They could make a marvellous collection. A memorial.'

'Wouldn't it be too much for you?'

'A memorial so that his writing didn't entirely disappear.'

Margaret said, 'His father always thought he would write books.'

The work filled Anna's thoughts and her evenings. She knew exactly what to do. She had been lucky in finding an address book among the papers, and she wrote to all the people who seemed to be friends. She heard after a time from about two thirds of them. The replies were all the same. They could not believe that he was dead – so young, talented, full of charming ideas. They were an odd medley of friends, from a Paris concierge to a Dutch artist in Rome, and most of them had stories of him. Tristram had spent a night on the Acropolis, visited Lourdes to watch the people's faces, picked his route along the Pilgrims' Way to Canterbury.

He had also travelled far more widely than Anna had known – to Russia and Israel but never to America. Some of the letters were difficult to decipher, but Anna went to the aunts for help in translation. She also took them some photographs that she had found among the letters. One was of a young Tristram in a blue shirt standing by a bridge parapet looking down at the Seine, with Notre Dame in the background. She thought that this might make a cover picture.

After a week or two it became clear that she could not go on working at the Hampstead house. It had to be sold. So she took a farewell look at Tristram's room, and desk and papers were transferred to her flat. But she still went out to the aunts to report progress.

She hesitated about going to Laurence for a contribution. He had said that doctors do not report private talks. But with the book she had no pride. She must gather all she could. So she sent him a note by Jack telling him of the book but adding, 'If you don't want to report anything I shall understand.'

She had not seen him since she had returned, and she had been so busy picking up her Fleet Street work that she had hardly noticed. Her mother had urged her to go to the doctor if she ever felt unwell, but somehow the book had given her a goal and she was feeling almost normal. She had been helped by the welcome from her office. Those fatherly men seemed glad to see 'little Miss Dean' back.

The doctor answered at once with almost half a page. He went back to the time, long before, when Tristram and Anna had been passing his surgery and Tristram had gone back to ask what doctors thought of death. Laurence briefly mentioned the last meeting as well. 'He wanted to know what a doctor's life was like and if I enjoyed it.' Finally Laurence quoted a typical fanciful Tristram remark – that everyone is an orchestra with many instruments playing but most people are aware only of the tune.

For nearly three months Anna worked on the book, gathering the anecdotes and writing a short biography and then assembling Tristram's best writing in sections. The title was to be just his name and dates, but it seemed to Anna that wherever you opened it there was something delightful. She wrote to Helena for the name of her publishers, and Helena got into touch with the firm and it promised to look out for the book. Anna began to make another selection in the hope of a second volume.

But then came a shock. In three weeks' time her typescript, neatly packed, came back. The firm agreed that it had some fine writing but they had decided that the 'readership' would not be enough to cover the cost of production. In these hard times to write well was hardly enough. The subject of such a memorial work should be known in some way, and Tristram Forrest seemed to be unknown. He had never been on television, had he?

Anna, indignant, rang up Helena and said that some illiterate fool must have got hold of the book. Helena agreed that publishers' judgment depended very much on the taste of individual readers. She gave Anna more publishers' names, and Anna sent the book round to one after the other. Each time it came back, sometimes with a letter and sometimes with just a rejection slip.

Anna was tearing at the latest rejection packet when Jack came in one evening. He still did small jobs for her and still talked interminably, but she generally listened because he wanted an audience and she was grateful. But that evening when he began on his saga of the Atlantic she could bear no more but savagely slit up the cardboard of the packet, read the rejection slip and said, 'What's the use of talking about the Atlantic? It would be a good thing if the human race *were* drowned.'

Jack went on for a minute; then realised that she was objecting and stopped. He said mildly, 'There's some good people in the world, miss.'

'Good!' Anna said. 'All they care about is profit, money, pandering to the multitude.'

Jack had no idea of what she was talking about. He protested, 'I've seen some fantastic rescues.'

'Oh stop talking about rescues,' she cried. 'I'm talking about the mind, taste, how it's rotten in England. They don't care, these business people. They know nothing of culture, writing or anything else. It makes me despair.'

Jack looked puzzled, said 'Sorry' and went out quietly.

Late that evening the doctor rang up. She felt guilty because she had not seen him since her return. After all he had been kind in her illness. Now he was being careful of her again. He said, 'Jack thinks you are ill.'

She was glad to talk to somebody. 'I'm not. I'm just fed up. The Tristram book has come back a fifth time.'

'What's wrong with it?'

'Tristram wasn't a TV hero. The fools say that it wouldn't have a wide enough readership.'

He said, 'I suppose one should have expected it,' and then made the suggestion that was to rescue her. 'Have you ever thought of having it printed privately?'

She had not. She had just thought that if a book were good it automatically was printed somehow. But Laurence had surprised her once or twice before with his general information, and now he told her that doctors knew a little about publishing as works that had no public appeal appeared without the help of the popular firms. He even, it appeared during that long conversation, knew the name of a printer who might take on the work.

'It would be expensive, of course. I suppose I might contribute something.'

Anna said, 'His aunts have been very pleased at the idea.'

'Would they help?'

'I don't know. They've just sold the house.'

She was going out to Hampstead the following Saturday, but she could not wait. She telephoned to Hampstead and poured out her troubles and Laurence's suggestion to Margaret Forrest. Margaret said briefly, 'It's no good expecting much of the business world, my dear. I'll speak to Beatrice.'

Anna said, 'Laurence thinks he might help. I could add something if we waited a bit.'

Margaret came back. 'We'd prefer not to wait too long, my dear. We're both in our seventies, and we would like to see the book before we go. Tell the printer to send the bill to us.'

The printer seemed anxious to oblige Anna because she knew Dr Gregg. With her co-operation the book could be produced in a month or so. He suggested printing a few hundred copies first – enough for friends, a few local libraries and serious journals. He thought that the Paris photograph would make a good cover, but objected that just Tristram's name and dates were too short for a title. So Anna added, 'Wandering and Watching'.

So there was peace at the end of the summer, and it was a boundless relief not to dread the postman's knock. Laurence joined in discussions, and the two did not always agree. He, as a scientist, preferred long paragraphs and modest headings. She, as a journalist, wanted short paragraphs and more display. The printer generally agreed with Anna, but Laurence excelled in proof-reading. Anna

Anna With Tristram

continued to go through the remains of Tristram's papers. She found a small piece of verse entitled 'Anna' but it was so scored through and altered that she could not read it. Only one phrase was clear – 'implacable tenderness'.

Rose had two things to decide – if the Careys really wanted her and, if they did, how she would behave. She sat in her Yorkshire office and was happy but uncertain.

After two years away it could not be the same. She had experienced different industries, social prides, scenery, voices. Here in Yorkshire had been problems in the textile industry and in mining communities, whereas in the Midlands the industries had been much more varied and in Worcestershire she had had to deal with rural poverty. But she had found the Yorkshire people warm-hearted and she would have been content to stay; only she missed Ladyhill and the children who were growing up and all The Hollies family.

She had spent holidays with them and settled back into old ways. She still wrote weekly to Edward. But there had been all this new experience which they did not share, and she felt sometimes that she was losing touch with them; that the things that she could talk about meant little to them. Except for Edward, of course. He was always interested in social problems.

Something else had happened up here in Yorkshire. She had acquired an adorer. For the first time in her life she had become a goddess. She was used to keeping in the background and looking with admiration on others. But now Phyl, the big former schoolgirl aged nineteen, gazed at her with loving eyes while the rest of the office laughed.

Phyl, who was coming into the office for work experience while she was taking a social-welfare course, had been given a table in Rose's room, and Rose had naturally helped her. And soon had begun those bunches of flowers, invitations to tea at the suburban talkative home, offers to clean Rose's car, even a watch on her birthday. All this had intensely embarrassed her.

She had come to realise that the person who is adored is a victim. He cannot behave naturally. He has to receive gushing compliments and be grateful. Still Rose had borne the situation for months, with the amused comments of colleagues, and she would have gone on bearing it; only the Birmingham appointment had intervened.

She had noticed the advertisement in a social-service journal and at the last moment for obscure reasons had applied. She had not expected to get the appointment, but anything connected with Birmingham interested her, and she had trained in the city and knew some of the staff. It was foolish really, as she was happy in Yorkshire, and afterwards she had wished she had not bothered. All the same perhaps, deep down, was the feeling that the Midlands were home.

She had been surprised to be summoned for an interview, and the other candidates whom she had met had had more experience. She had been easy at the interview because she had expected nothing, but she had met some old acquaintances. She had not been out to Ladyhill because she had to return immediately to some difficult cases of suspected child neglect which she had to review for the Yorkshire committee. Her pleasure at seeing the Birmingham people was mixed with thoughts of the next day's work as she returned north. She wrote to Edward that night, 'I've made a flying visit to Birmingham but had to rush back. It was about a vague sort of job, but it had no results.'

But she had written too soon. The next morning had come the call at her office. She was offered the Birmingham appointment, and for the moment she was dazzled. Back, back to where she belonged – Edward, the children, the gardens. She saw a vision of Ladyhill in summer with its cottage flower-beds and hills in the distance, and for the moment she had never been so happy.

But then the hard part had begun. She had to announce her coming departure and take the congratulations but laments of the office. She realised that she had been popular, which surprised her; that she had made many friends and that there would be losses too in going south.

And now here was the problem of Phyl. The great girl had come in in the middle of the morning, had heard the news, had burst into the room and now was actually dabbing her eyes. And Rose, who had been protective and kind to her for months, had to change her tactics. More kindness would have meant more tears.

Rose said, 'I'm very sorry. I didn't know it was going to happen. But it may be a good thing. You have to learn to be independent; to stand on your own two feet.'

Suddenly, as she spoke, she felt that she was quoting someone else. 'Be independent. Stand on your own feet.' It was Edward, of course.

He had preached the same sermon to her.

She had not been abject like Phyl. She had taken his advice and left Ladyhill. But she remembered with shame how she was in the habit of pouring out her praise and compliments to the eccentric figure who had become a tutor to her, and how he had not liked them and had laughed or changed the subject.

She had thought that she had bestowed some benefit on him by her praise, but now she knew how uncomfortable it was to be adored, and she was afraid – that Edward would not want her back and Helena might not want her either, with the way she, Rose, hung on Edward's words. She had invited herself back. Suppose that, in secret, they had been glad to be rid of her.

She took an easy way out with Phyl. 'Of course I'll write, but, you know, you'll soon find somebody else. You'll get a boyfriend. You'll get married. You won't want to bother with me any more.'

And Phyl blew her nose and quieted. She was nineteen and the future was before her. But Rose had become a successful professional woman with many friends but only one deep emotional relationship. And she might have made herself a nuisance with that. She did not know.

She wrote almost apologetically to Edward that evening. 'I shall get a flat in Birmingham of course, and I shall understand if you haven't time for the old week-ends. I've learned up here to live an independent life, and I feel that I may have depended too much on you in the past.'

The result was a telephone call from Edward two evenings later. 'What a splendid bombshell. But, heavens above, Rose, are you getting too grand for us? Of course the old room is still waiting for you if you want to come at week-ends.'

That reassured her a little, but she was still cautious when she announced that she was coming down to Birmingham at the week-end to look for a flat. 'I shall have a lot to do, and you all may be busy too. Let me know if it's not convenient.'

The result was another call from Edward. 'What's come over you?'

'Only trying not to be a nuisance.'

'A nuisance! You!'

She found a suitable Birmingham flat quite quickly, and after the business had a solitary lunch listening to the old Birmingham voices but a little uneasy at the changes in the centre of the city. But after all her mind was on Ladyhill, and she took the familiar bus out through the suburbs. It was the end of August but she had not yet had a summer holiday so that she had not seen The Hollies for some months.

But it was all the same – the scattered red houses, the banks with small yellow flowers, the hedges with their brambles. For a moment it seemed as if the Yorkshire interim had never existed, but then she reminded herself that she must be careful. Be willing to withdraw at any moment. Still they might not want her.

Millie opened the door, her face red from cooking. 'Now isn't it lovely? You'll be able to make some more of your little rock cakes for us. Leave your bag. Helena's in the garden.'

The house had the usual scent of polish and apples. Rose went out at the back, past the beds of dahlias and asters to the lawn. The grass was scattered with a rug, balls, bits of paper and a toy rabbit. Irene was sitting drawing as usual, and Helena was beside her while the baby was picking up leaves and throwing them at her. Kate had grown almost into a little girl. Prancing about she gave the impression of energy and concentration with a spice of acting. 'Naughty,' she cried while Helena brushed herself down.

Helena said, 'I shall never get these bits out of my hair.' She looked dishevelled and brown. 'Stop it,' she said to Kate and then to Rose, 'My God, I'm pleased to see you. We want a devoted aunt here.'

Rose stood looking down on them and saw days of service ahead, amusement without limit. But she was still cautious. 'Are you sure that you can do with an extra person?' But then Irene broke in in her grave way. 'I've done a picture for your room. It's trees with a little cuckoo in the middle.'

Helena said, 'Talking of cuckoos, Jenny has been singing "Land of Hope and Glory" since she heard you were coming back. We'll have tea in a moment when Jos gets back from the pottery. Edward's planting bulbs. He's been looking out for you.'

'Safe there,' Rose thought with relief. 'In the glass-house,' Helena said and Rose went across. Edward was standing at the end of one of the glass-houses planting bulbs with pots and bags around him. She saw him over a haze of ferns and foliage, and it was a pleasure to watch him. He looked up and she said 'I'm here,' and he said, 'It's nearly tea-time.' It was as if they were continuing a past conversation. She stood by him and said, 'I'm in trouble with a girl up there.'

'Obstreperous?'

'Too fond of me.'

'Very odd,' he said, looking at her sideways.

'Don't laugh. Don't you think that too much affection can be a burden?'

'I don't know, never having had too much of it.'

'You know you've always preached independence.'

'Have I?' He seemed to have forgotten.

'And I've always tried to follow your advice.'

'So now you don't want to come near us.'

'I wish you *sometimes* wouldn't make jokes.'

'You've grown waspish,' he said.

She was thinking, 'Home again and nothing to worry about. Why was I so frightened?' In the old days she would have said something like, 'It's marvellous to see you,' but she held back remembering her lecture to Phyl.

'I've grown independent,' she said.

He dusted his hands and took his stick. 'Well don't stop coming here anyway.'

It had been a disastrous day. One of Millie's old cats had been found dead in a cupboard, and Jos was in London so Edward had to bury it. It was raining and he got wet and his rheumatism began to plague him, and Irene, who had come out to put flowers on the grave, got her hair wet. Then Helena, who almost was never cross with Irene, scolded her because she might get a cold just when she was going back to school.

There was the Ladyhill flower-show at the end of the week. The rain would spoil the flowers, including Edward's roses and dahlias, but a last committee meeting was being held at the Ploughman's Arms, and Edward tramped through the rain to it and made his knee even worse. Crabby was left to dig a bed of potatoes and came in caked with mud and sneezing, and Millie sent him home.

The children had to play in the music room. Jenny came in as usual, but she cried with Millie over the cat and, being upset, slapped Kate for throwing a shoe at her. Kate bawled, and Helena came down from her room where she was trying to read the proofs of her new book on the Lunar Society. She had been slow with the proofs and the publishers had written asking for them. She was always a little on edge when Jos was away, and now stood silent at the door while the baby howled and clawed at her skirt. Helena was always scrupulously polite to Jenny now, but she said coldly, 'You've almost done your two hours. You can finish now if you like,' and Jenny went out looking glum.

Then Irene did not want her dinner, either because of the death of the cat or the uproar. Kate was supposed to have an afternoon rest while Irene sat quietly with a book, but the baby somehow let down the side of her cot, climbed out and butted into Helena's room where she was busy with her proofs. It was too late to put Kate back to sleep, and Helena came down and decided to lengthen a skirt for Irene, but could not find her scissors. It turned out that Irene had given them to Crabby who had lost his and wanted to cut his nails. At this Helena muttered something about needing the patience of Job, and tears rolled down Irene's cheeks. Helena, instead of comforting her as she generally would have done, said to Edward, 'I'm losing my temper. Can you look after them for a bit?' and retired upstairs.

Edward was used to looking after the children for brief spells, but now it was more than half an hour to tea. He got out the family box of bricks, and Irene helped by building castles for Kate to knock down. In the middle Kate escaped to the kitchen, found a bag of flour and dribbled it over the surviving cat. Millie chased her out and then came in to say that Helena wondered if he would mind for once if she had her tea in her room because of the proofs. Edward said, 'We'll manage,' and Kate knocked over her mug of milk.

The sun emerged just when it was too late to go out or do anything in the garden. Edward amused the children by making rabbit shadows with his hands on the wall, and looked many timed at the clock. At last Helena called from above, and he kissed the two children and could lie back and close his eyes.

The telephone went several times and Millie answered it. Then she came in to say that a boy at Meadow Grange had chickenpox and the warden was sorry, but he thought the opening of the leisure centre would have to be postponed. Edward said, 'I'll ring him tomorrow,' and began to clear up the children's muddle. Then he sat down to type letters but stopped in the middle of the first. He was worried about Helena.

He had worried about her in the old days when he was in charge. After her marriage he was free of the responsibility, but he had got into the habit of concerning himself about her, especially when Jos was away. She looked younger now than she had done ten years before, but she was having broken nights and long days with the children, as well as trying to continue with her books. Could she stand it?

Bumps and shrieks came from above. Then Helena was singing, and then there were calls as Irene had her bath. The two children were now together in Edward's old room and he had moved to be away from the noise. At times he was glad of his haven of peace.

But now silence descended – the solid silence that comes after children go to sleep – but Helena did not come down. Edward typed a few letters and switched on the electric fire. Evenings were growing chilly and soon winter would come with its long darkness and children's coughs.

It was nearly eight when Helena appeared and Millie brought in the supper tray. Helena flung herself into an armchair, and Edward, who had been half asleep, said, 'Are you dead?' The house was quiet now, and the thought came to him that here, for once, were the two original Careys alone together after all the changes and the new figures. Twenty years before the two had been alone except for old Mary the housekeeper and the baby Benedict. Now the house was full of new life and the two of them almost never sat alone together. This evening was like old times.

Perhaps Helena too felt this relaxation of the past. She was lying back and smiling. 'Goodness,' she answered. 'No. They were little saints tonight. Kate went down without a murmur after being awake this afternoon. I was the limit to leave them so long with you.'

'I've been wondering if Kate was too much for you.'

'You needn't worry. I get mad with her sometimes, but I'd be lost without her. So would Irene. I could always get somebody in if I wanted, but with Jenny and Rose now at week-ends . . .'

'Everything's all right.'

'Of course nothing is ever perfect. But I suppose I'm happier than I've ever been. Oh and Jos has rung up and has sold some pots and is coming back tomorrow. And I've done twenty pages of proofs.'

But this talk was to be different from the old ones. In the past it had always been Helena's welfare that had been important. Edward had been the guardian, whose own personal life was hardly mentioned. But now Helena was free, able to turn her mind to other people. She said suddenly, 'Have you ever thought of marrying Rose?'

'Of course I have.'

'Then why don't you? She'd be glad.'

'Not now, I think. She has got her career, and she keeps on talking about independence.'

'If you showed you wanted her she'd come like a shot.'
'I'm too old,' he said.
'You're not. Pater was thirty years older than my mother.'
'He wasn't a bachelor with rheumatism.'

She looked at him solicitously as she seldom had before. 'You're not feeling ill, are you?'

'Only old. I can remember you being born.'

She said, 'I suppose most of my childhood memories are mixed up with the trips down here, and the pickabacks and the botany books.'

They looked at one another, and Edward vaguely realised why he had never made Rose more than a friend. She, Helena, had always been there at the centre of his life and she always would be. 'You're an odd creature,' she said, 'but I've always done pretty well out of you.'

'If you're happy...' he said.
'I am, more or less.'
'Then I am too.'

By the end of October the Tristram book was finished – almost a year after his death. In a way it had saved Anna and staved off the future. She wondered what Tristram himself would have thought of it. Though he had so seldom talked of himself he must have known that he had the gift of writing that took one's breath away. And had practised his art and left all those crumpled pages behind. He might have laughed, Anna thought, but he would have been pleased.

As for herself, she had learnt many new things from the venture. Its chief gift, of course, had been the experience of the writings themselves, but also there had been all those friends involved. She had come across some odd characters and had glimpses into unexpected places. She thought, 'People seem to grow confidential when there is a death.'

But the discoveries had not been only about Tristram's scattered friends. Working with somebody, you develop a special intimate relationship, especially if you are discussing human experiences. Anna and Laurence had co-operated before – on the affairs of Mrs Noakes, Carol, the baby – but now they had regular sessions together to discuss the arrangement and meaning of words, and, though they argued and disagreed, their arguments sometimes spilled over into personal matters.

Anna With Tristram

They had included the surgery itself. In asserting the need for an attractive book, Anna accused Laurence of not using his eyes enough. 'Look at your waiting-room – those dingy cream walls and brown floor covering. Wouldn't your patients feel better with brighter colours and a picture or two as well as all those leaflets?' He said, 'I know I don't notice such things enough. Never been trained. Perhaps you'd advise me,' and she was pleased in a way because she so bitterly missed Tristram's talks on art.

She thought now that Laurence's air of authority hid some deep timidity, but he was aware of this and very much in control of himself. In their arguments he was the reasonable one, and this sometimes humiliated her. She wished that sometimes he would show a little temper.

Tristram's aunts, who had helped with the reminiscences and money, were different too. They had seemed kindly old sisters living in peace with themselves and their neighbours. They had not shown a great deal of emotion when Tristram died. But, as she went out almost weekly, Anna became aware of a darker side. Their lives had been wrecked by the war, and their intellectual friends, many of them Jewish, had been destroyed. They had returned to England almost as strangers, made a new life for themselves and been useful to their brother and nephew. But now these had gone too.

But they were women born just before the turn of the century and reflected the intellectual climate of the time – agnostics who after the two wars expected little of life. They did not inflict their emotions on other people, but they were lonely and gradually, it seemed, Anna was becoming a blessing to them. In the end she was talking freely to them and they were begging her to come again almost as she had begged Tristram. It was a strange transfer.

Now at last the shiny volumes with the picture of Tristram had arrived and Anna had only to distribute them. This work staved off the emptiness of the future, but she cherished that other plan behind – the shadowy child who would hold out its arms to her.

First Laurence must have a copy. She took a book across. Through the summer they had grown friendly and she did not hesitate now to go to the surgery. Now he only glanced at the book; they had been through it so many times already, but he seemed pleased. 'You've made a good job of it. What will you do with your evenings now?'

The question was amiable enough, but then suddenly, out of nothing, a quarrel blew up. Anna said 'I'm going to write articles to make more money.'

He knew what the money was for and said, trading on their intimacy, 'Anna, couldn't you drop this idea of adoption?'

This ruffled her. It was her only shield. 'Why should I?'

'Tristram didn't approve.'

'How do you know?'

He was silent, and she remembered that he had refused to tell her what Tristram had said. She became excited. 'You won't tell me. Did he want me to go on year after year for fifty years with nothing?'

'No. He didn't want that. He wanted you to have more experience.'

'Experience!' and her grief burst out. 'Haven't I had enough experience? One death is enough.'

He said mildly, 'It need not be of death,' but she turned on him. She had never criticised him to his face before, but now she was goaded by grief. 'Experience! And what experience have you had? Living alone in a gloomy house with only an old man to talk to.'

Now he too stiffened. 'I am not discussing myself.'

'But I am. You doctors criticise and try to rule our lives, and we can't criticise back.' Then she heard Jack's door open upstairs and knew that she had been shouting. She was penitent and said, 'Sorry. Why do you stir me up? If you were a little less – less wooden.' She saw his tight lips; said 'Sorry' again, and walked out.

Afterwards she was discouraged and ashamed. He made no difference to her adoption plan, of course, but there probably would be a great deal of criticism. As for Laurence himself, she had been rude and unjust. She had better keep away in future, she thought, and in the next few days, as she did parcels up in the evenings, she was depressed and went through the old pain of missing Tristram.

She had to take the book out to Hampstead on the Saturday. She carried out six copies, not expecting much – only their affection and the sight of the brown eyes that were like his. But then the unexpected happened, and the world became quite different.

The aunts too only glanced at the book. 'We'll study it when you've gone,' Margaret said, and Anna knew that this was because of their reserve. She heard a tremble in the aunt's voice and changed the subject, talking of her own doings. The quarrel with Laurence was on her mind, and she said, 'I've just had an argument with my doctor friend.'

'Dr Gregg?' Margaret said. 'I thought him very agreeable.'

Anna was surprised. 'You don't know him, do you?'

'He was in touch at Tristram's death. He gave us many useful details.'

So here was still more praise for Laurence, and he had given them details which he refused to her, Anna. She was piqued and said, 'He's abominably conventional.'

Conventional? How? She had to explain, and over the lavish tea-table the future plan came out. Anna expected cries of disapproval, but then she realised that the aunts were listening with flushed cheeks, and Beatrice said, 'Good girl. This is admirable.'

Anna stayed late that evening talking of her plan and hearing of their return to England in 1939. In a curious way the two themes came together for the aunts seemed haunted by the idea that they might have brought with them one or two of those little intelligent girls who had been left to perish. Of course they did not know at the time of the coming destruction, and it might have been impossible to bring such children to England. But they had not even tried, and now they were troubled with regrets. 'If we had made the effort then we should not have been such lonely old women now.'

In the end Beatrice asked, 'How will you pay for your child?'

'I shall have to save for a long time.'

They had already paid for the book, but now Beatrice, as the older sister, began to talk of money again. 'We have a little. There is no-one now to inherit it. If it could be of any use to you . . .'

But then Anna, taken aback, thanked them many times but was frightened. The child of the future had been very far away, but now the plan came close and was certain. 'I can't do it yet,' she protested, and they said, 'Of course not, but the money could be there when you need it.'

When she left they said, 'You'll keep in touch, won't you, my dear. You'll continue to visit us.' And Anna said, 'How could I otherwise?' If she had been told a year before that such an intimacy would develop she would not have believed it.

That evening, returning in the train – the train always hallowed because Tristram had used it – she held an imaginary conversation with him. 'Your aunts are wiser than you were, and they've made me happy.' But it was not exactly happiness; more like shouldering a burden that was inescapable and yet welcome. It was peace too. She knew what her future was going to be.

Edward's leisure centre opened at the beginning of November when the chickenpox at Meadow Grange was over. The opening was later than he had hoped, but the centre would be ready for the winter when it would be most needed. He had arranged for a few posters to be put up round the village, but crowds more people had come than he had expected. Fortunately, it was a sunny afternoon with dry roads.

A line of cars was parked outside the centre. The four firms which had given funds had sent representatives. The Council had sent two women, and there were two reporters from local papers. Some farmers had come, and Dr Gregg had driven down with Alan from London. Edward found it strange that he himself had engendered all this activity.

He had had, of course, many helpers. Meadow Grange had been cleaned and tidied and now the boys in their best clothes were taking people round both home and centre. Jos and Crabby were receiving people who came across to The Hollies and wanted to see the gardens. Helena and Millie were making tea for guests to the house. In the small kitchen of the centre Rose was serving more tea. Benedict and Jenny were presiding over the 'museum' that Jenny had insisted on having. It consisted of a large table supplied by one of the villagers and suitably of antique oak. The exhibits included a piece of Roman tile found near Jos's pottery, the stone head of a garden cherub from Ken Burrows's junk yard, a pile of Jenny's albums with pressed flowers, photographs of the church and other old buildings sent by the vicar and two white-grey strands of hair from Frost, the pony that had lived in the field for so long. Jenny had tied them with blue ribbons and written a memorial notice. She had also written labels neatly and an invitation to anybody who had anything 'funny or of great interest' to bring it along.

The Deans had arrived from Birmingham, and Edward went out to speak to Hughie and his father who had sacrificed an afternoon of television sport. Edward had sometimes wondered how Agnes Dean could have settled down with a works manager, but he found the Dean father good-natured, sensible and on easy terms with Hughie. The boy had decided to keep on with his car business and remain out of the family firm. 'It's a bit of a jolt,' the father said, 'but Agnes and I aren't dead yet, and I've got one or two good lads I can train up in management.'

Village children were clustered round the car's open bonnet while Hughie explained the mechanism. Occasionally he would pack several children in and take them for a short ride while explaining the gears. The ground round the car was sprinkled with dropped crisps and packets, and the Dean father produced a brush and a plastic bag from the car and told one of the boys to clear up. Edward liked his air of genial authority. 'You're more used to controlling lads than I am,' Edward said. He had given up teaching classes some years before.

He went back to the centre and shook hands with the vicar who hoped he might borrow the hall sometimes. Mrs Owen and Gran were there, and told him that Frank had to stay in the shop and Alan had gone to talk to him. It was now four o'clock, and Edward had been greeting people since 2.30. He was tired of being told that he was 'wonderful' or 'wonderful for your age' and his knee began to hurt. He said to Rose, 'I'm going home for a little. I'll be there if anybody wants me,' and quietly opened the swing doors and breathed the fresh wind. With a feeling of guilt he stumped across to The Hollies, found the front door open and dropped into the big chair in the dining-room.

He could hear Helena and Millie washing up in the kitchen and some droning song from the music room. Otherwise there was blessed calm. He was melancholy for some reason – because it was the end of effort, because he had been called wonderful so many times and because Mr Dean had been so good at controlling the boys.

He thought of Mrs Noakes's home crowded with old people who were no good to God or man – useless, waiting to die as he would now be. He dozed and dreamed that he was at the door of The Hollies but some stranger would not let him in saying, 'You're no more use.'

Then there were voices in the room. Rose was with a haggard-looking woman whom he had often seen about the village. She came from the housing estate and was reputed to have a drunken, unemployed husband and a son who had left school but also had no work, and belonged to a gang in trouble with the Police.

Rose said, 'Mrs Flack has been looking for you. Will you have a word with her?'

Edward, hazy from sleep, thought, 'Not another!' But he could not be rude, and he asked the woman, 'Have you had a cup of tea?'

She had, of course, and Rose said, 'Can I leave you? We're still hard at work over there.' The woman stood waiting, and Edward pulled himself together and asked her to sit down. Then he had to listen to a flood of distress. Her husband was spending the family allowance on drink, and her son had fights with him. They owed weeks of rent and there was often not enough to eat. And casual harvesting jobs such as apple-picking were over. There were no brussels-sprouts fields near, and her son would not use his bike to ride four miles to the nearest field.

Edward guessed that she had come to ask for a loan but was ashamed. He knew perfectly well that it is demoralising to give money to a beggar. All the same, she was worried and poor, and he was not, and life was unfair. Luckily he had left some cash in a sideboard drawer, and he pushed himself up and went to it. He did not know what to give her, but he took out twenty pounds in notes and said, 'I'm afraid it isn't much.'

She went red and said, 'I'll pay you back as soon as I can,' though they both knew that she never would, but would probably come back for more. The notes would not make any difference to the situation anyhow, but she might, he thought, get a little pleasure from them.

He waited for her to go, but she lingered. 'I wondered if, you being one of the chief men of the village, if you'd have a word with my son.'

Edward, weary, said, 'What good would that do?'

'It might frighten him a bit – you inviting him up here. You could talk to him about jobs and tell him to behave hisself.'

'I'm very busy,' Edward said, then he remembered that he would not be as busy in future. Then he thought of his own adolescence with his mother dead and his father critical, and he yielded. 'Oh well, send him up. But let me know when.'

Still she looked at him timidly. 'There's a lot of people on the estate that needs a bit of advice. My neighbour's got a spastic daughter. And there's no Citizens' Bureau round here for us to go to.'

'I can't talk to everyone on the estate,' Edward protested.

'No sir. But we wondered, some of us, if you could have a little office at the centre to give advice-like. Open it once a week.'

There it was, something that might be useful, and he had never thought of it. He looked at her with more respect. 'It's an idea.'

'We get all them papers,' said Mrs Flack, 'and we don't understand half of them. If somebody could help us we might get a bit more money.'

He had not thought of it, yet he had always felt that more contact should be made with the estate. He sat up. He was not as tired as he had thought. He began to consider names for a panel. 'It may be a good idea,' he said to Mrs Flack. 'I'll let you know.'

Five minutes later Helena looked in. 'Has some woman from the

Anna With Tristram

estate been bothering you? Are you all right? Why, you're smiling all over your face.'

Anna hoped to avoid the doctor. Old Jack had told her that he was invited to the opening, but she expected there would be a crowd in which she could hide. She was serene now. She knew her future. But Laurence did not approve and she did not want any more quarrels.

There was certainly a crowd there when she and her mother went through the swing doors. She was small and could stay quietly in a corner, she thought. Almost at once Rose Webb was there, flushed and thanking people. She took Mrs Dean's arm. 'I'm so glad to see you. I need help with the tea. I'm swamped.' People were crowding round saying, 'How splendid to have you back. Do drop in one evening,' and Rose embarrassed kept saying, 'Have some tea.' Mrs Dean said to Anna, 'Have a wander round. I'll see you later at The Hollies,' and she went to help at the tea counter.

It was a chance for Anna to keep away from Laurence. She followed a boy from Meadow Grange who was acting as a guide. He conducted one or two people upstairs to see the games and television rooms and magazine corner with a pile of *Country Life* sent by the Ploughman's Arms. She spent a few minutes turning over the magazines, but some more people came up and she had to move on. Then, cautiously descending the open stairway, she saw Laurence below talking to her mother. She paused feeling trapped, but Jenny came and pulled his sleeve to take him to the museum.

Anna seized the chance of escape. She slipped through the crowd and opened the back door. Here were the seats that Edward had placed to give a view down the field to the hollow at the bottom with its yellow autumn trees. And, as so often, Anna tried to imagine what Tristram would have made of the scene – the crowded warm hall with its chatter and then the chilly silence outside. A metaphor for life and afterwards? But perhaps that was too obvious for Tristram. Perhaps he would have written only about the green slope and the sunset.

She imagined his voice saying the old dreaded, 'I must go,' but now she did not protest. It was all too peaceful. In imagination she saw him standing on the crest and then wandering slowly down the slope.

He had never been to Ladyhill and she had failed to find him in his Hampstead room, but now she imagined his face very clearly. Still in imagination she saw him far down the slope and then vanishing among the trees, and she thought, 'Thank God. One more glimpse.'

She was cold, but she did not want to go back to the centre. She skirted the garden and went out by the Meadow Grange gate. There were people in the road but she did not know them, and she did not speak to them but went up to The Hollies where the door was ajar. From the music room came a child's drone. 'Eh diggle diggle. Eh diggle diggle.'

Anna peered in. Irene was sitting on the floor reading a book that had probably been given her by a visitor. Kate, in a green party dress with a full skirt, was in the centre of the room droning the song and dancing. She held a rubber duck and stretched her arms wide and turned in circles. She seemed completely involved in her own movements.

She saw Anna, looked at her sideways and began to sway to and fro waving the duck. She was showing off, of course, but she was no longer the demanding violent baby. She was a performer, enjoying herself on her own.

But then Anna became aware that she was trapped after all. Laurence must have seen her in the road and followed her. But she was absorbed in watching this new Kate, and she did not mind. She said, 'Do you remember two years ago? It's unbelievable.'

Irene had looked up and was watching smiling. She had always been proud of the baby's antics. Kate, with all the eyes on her, increased her performance, throwing the duck up, missing it and snatching it from the floor.

Anna said, 'Could you have believed that the wet bundle would turn to this?'

As they all watched Laurence said, apparently without rancour, 'I've been looking for you. Miss Forrest telephoned.'

'Margaret? Why ever should she?'

'She seemed to think I was discouraging you.'

'You can't. It's all settled. They're going to help me.'

It was the same old argument, but Kate's dance seemed to have taken away the bitterness. 'Of course,' he said, 'no-one is going to compel you in any way.'

'Did she say that?'

'No, I did.'

'Eh diggle.' Kate came dancing forward and threw the duck at the doctor.

'Look. Look how extraordinary children are,' Anna said. 'Don't you see why I want one?'

'There are other ways.'

Suddenly she groped at a suspicion. 'Is that what Tristram said to you?'

He did not answer but she persisted. 'When he came to talk about me? Did he ask you . . . ?'

'Eh diggle.' Kate lunged forward and clawed at Anna's skirt. Anna lifted her and she swung round and seized Laurence's shoulder. 'Eh diggle. The cat and the figgle.' For one moment they were linked and Anna felt the warm human contact that she had lacked for so long. Then the baby slithered down, and she and the doctor faced each other. Some spark had sprung up – curiosity, doubt, perhaps final understanding.

'*Did* Tristram suggest that?'

'Only if it would make you happy.'

Kate began her dance again. 'Eh diggle. Eh diggle. An' de dish man amay wiv de poon.'

* Droz.com

* Dragonsdenshopping.com

* ageless male.com

* safeway.ca